PUP AT THE PALACE

"Where is he?" Mandy cried desperately, looking around. Normally, she'd have loved to watch the mounted guards riding past on their sleek, beautifully groomed black horses. But now all she could think about was the little animal. She hated to think of him being trampled under the horses' hooves or running out into the road and getting knocked over by a car. "James, we have to find the puppy quickly!"

"I can't see him anywhere!" he shouted back, already separated from Mandy by a crowd of people. "He seems to have vanished!"

Frantically, they looked down and searched through the forest of legs around them for any sign of the pup. But it was hopeless — there was no trace of the little dog.

"Let's go and find Mom and Dad," Mandy called to James. "They can help us search. Come on, there's no time to lose!"

Give someone you love a home!
Read about the animals of Animal Ark™

PUP at the PALACE

Ben M. Baglio

Illustrations by Ann Baum

Cover illustration by
Mary Ann Lasher

AN
APPLE
PAPERBACK

SCHOLASTIC INC.
New York Toronto London Auckland Sydney
Mexico City New Delhi Hong Kong Buenos Aires

ISBN 0-439-34391-7

All rights reserved. Published by Scholastic Inc., 557 Broadway, New York, NY 10012, by arrangement with Working Partners Limited. ANIMAL ARK is a trademark of Working Partners Limited. SCHOLASTIC, APPLE PAPERBACKS, and associated logos are trademarks and/or registered trademarks of Scholastic Inc.

12 11 10 9 8 7 6   2 3 4 5 6 7/0

Printed in the U.S.A.   40
First Scholastic printing, March 2002

To David Teale—a good friend to Animal Ark.

Special thanks to Jennie Walters.
Thanks also to C.J. Hall,
B.Vet.Med., M.R.C.V.S., for reviewing
the veterinary information contained in this book.

TM

One

"Can you see anything yet, James?" Mandy Hope called eagerly across the parking lot of the Fox and Goose. Pushing back her blond hair, she shaded her eyes against the early morning sun as she gazed over toward her friend.

"Not a sign," James replied, turning around from his lookout post by the side of the road. "Do you think they've forgotten about us?" he asked anxiously.

"Now, don't you go alarming everyone, James Hunter!" Mandy's grandmother, Dorothy Hope, said good-naturedly. "I called to check yesterday, and a bus

1

was definitely booked for eight o'clock. We've got a little while to wait until then."

"The driver won't dare to be a second late, if he knows
what's good for him," said her husband, Tom Hope,
smiling at Mandy. "You know what your grandmother's
like when she's in an organizing mood. Terrifying!"

As an active member of the Welford Women's Club,
Dorothy Hope had volunteered to arrange their summer
sight-seeing expedition to London. It would be a wonderful way to celebrate the new century, and everyone
was looking forward to seeing the Millennium Dome.

When Mandy had heard about the trip, she'd immediately thought it would be the perfect vacation for her
hardworking parents — not to mention herself! Emily
and Adam Hope had been frantically busy earlier in the
summer at Animal Ark, their veterinary practice in the
small Yorkshire village of Welford. Things had quieted
down a little, so they were taking a few days off and
leaving Simon, the clinic's nurse, in charge. They'd offered to take James to London along with them as his
parents couldn't get away just then.

"Is everyone here now, Grandma?" Mandy asked,
looking around the group that was waiting in the parking lot. She recognized lots of faces, though the people
she knew best were the pet owners who came to her
parents' clinic.

There was Mrs. Platt, whom Mandy had helped to adopt an abandoned poodle from the animal sanctuary. She had a son in London she wanted to visit, so she'd placed the little dog, Antonia, in a kennel and come along. Next to her stood Miss Davy, who lived in the Old Schoolhouse and kept a flock of hens in her large yard. She looked as immaculate as ever, from the top of her silvery-gray head to the tip of her shiny brown leather shoes. Beside her, Mrs. McFarlane from the post office was talking a mile a minute. Her husband was staying at home to look after their canary, Billy, and to keep the post office and shop running smoothly.

"Let me just find my list," said Mandy's grandmother, looking through the papers in her shoulder bag. "I think there are a few more people to come."

"You and that list!" teased her husband affectionately. "I think you must know it by heart, you've looked at it so many times."

"Well, you only have to put up with me and my list for a little while longer," Dorothy Hope replied sharply, pulling out a dog-eared sheet of paper. "Then you'll have total solitude for a few days."

"Now, come on, dear," Mandy's grandfather replied gruffly. "You know Smoky and I will be counting the days till you get back."

"Are you sure you won't be too lonely without us?"

Mandy asked him, suddenly picturing her grandfather and the cat all on their own in Lilac Cottage. She put her arm through his. "If you want to come along, I'm sure it's not too late."

Her grandfather shook his head. "I'd better not, honey," he replied. "The tomato plants in my green-house are at a very delicate stage, and they'll die for cer-tain if I leave them now. Don't you worry about me — your grandma's filled the freezer with food, and I'll be out in the garden from morning till night. I'll be expect-ing a postcard."

"I'll send you one of Buckingham Palace!" Mandy promised before rushing over to join James. She felt too excited to stand in one place for long.

James was still looking hopefully up the road.

"The bus should be coming soon!" Mandy said to him. "I can't wait to get going, can you?"

"No," James agreed, taking off his glasses and giving them a polish. "Though I hope Mom and Dad remember to take Blackie for lots of walks." He'd just said good-bye to his parents and given his excitable Labrador a big farewell hug. James spent a lot of time exercising Blackie and trying to train him, and Mandy knew he would miss his dog while they were away.

"We're going to have a great time," she said encouragingly, trying to take his mind off Blackie. "Just think of everything we'll be seeing — Buckingham Palace, Madame Tussaud's Wax Museum, Piccadilly Circus, the Tower of London —"

"And the Millennium Dome," James reminded her as he put his glasses back on, beginning to look a bit happier. "I really want to look at the computer displays in the Mind Zone."

"And you should get some great photos," Mandy said, spotting a camera at the top of James's bulging backpack. She knew how interested he was in photography.

"I didn't want to risk bringing my best camera along, so I've got the Polaroid," James told her. "Still, at least we can see the pictures right away. I just took one of Blackie so I'd have something to remind me of him while we're away." He pulled a photo out of his inside jacket pocket and showed it to Mandy.

"Oh, doesn't he look sweet!" Mandy said, smiling at Blackie's appealing face as he looked out of the picture with his head to one side. "Come on, let's go and show Mom and Dad. We might as well sit with them until the bus comes."

She picked up James's backpack for him and led the way over to where her parents were sitting on one of the benches outside the pub, chatting quietly together.

Her mother's long red hair glinted like a sheet of copper in the sun.

As they approached, her father broke into an enormous yawn, raising one hand up to his beard. "Don't worry, Dad," Mandy said, patting his knee as she sat down next to him. "You can have a good long sleep on the bus." She knew her father had been up most of the night, helping a cow that had had some difficulty giving birth.

"I can't wait," Dr. Adam replied, putting his hand over Mandy's. He looked paler than usual, and there were dark circles under his eyes. "I could do with a vacation now, that's for sure."

"Look at this great photo of Blackie that James has just taken," Mandy said, showing her parents the picture. "Doesn't he look cute?"

"He's got that wonderful Labrador grin on his face," her mother said. "They really do seem to smile sometimes, don't they?" She laughed and gave the photo back to James.

Dr. Emily and Dr. Adam loved animals just as much as Mandy did, and she often thought they must have the best job in the world. She'd learned a lot from helping them in the clinic, and one day she hoped to be as good a vet herself. The Hopes had adopted Mandy when she was a baby, and she couldn't imagine a better home than the one she'd found with them at Animal Ark.

They had only been sitting down for a few minutes when Mandy spotted what they'd all been waiting for. A white minibus was driving slowly down the Walton road. "At last!" she cried as it swung into the parking lot. "Now we can get moving!" She jumped to her feet and gave her father help getting up from the bench. Then she and James grabbed their backpacks, her father took the suitcase, and the four of them went over to join the others.

The driver opened the door and swung himself down, pushing a pair of sunglasses up on top of his head. "Glad you're all ready and waiting," he said as he unlocked the luggage compartment so the bags could be loaded in. "Traffic's building up already. I'll just pack the bags, and then we'll be off. Bill's the name, by the way." He was a small, energetic-looking man who obviously didn't believe in wasting time chatting.

"But there are two people who haven't arrived yet," Dorothy Hope told him, hurriedly consulting her list. "We can't go without them."

Bill looked at his watch. "Well, I can't wait forever," he said. "I promised to get you to London by two o'clock, so two o'clock sharp it'll be. I pride myself on my punctuality."

"Who else is coming?" Mandy asked her grandmother.

Before she could reply, James supplied Mandy with the answer. "Walter and Ernie!" he exclaimed in surprise.

Two elderly men were walking over from the short row of stone cottages behind the pub, each carrying a battered, ancient-looking suitcase.

"Ah, here they are," Dorothy Hope said with relief. "They must have been waiting at home till they saw the bus arrive."

"I'm surprised that they want to go to London," Mandy whispered to James. Walter Pickard and Ernie Bell lived a few doors apart from each other, and they both usually stayed close to home, apart from the occasional shopping trip into the nearby town of Walton.

"Morning, one and all," Walter said pleasantly as they approached, touching his flat cap in greeting. He was a large, gentle man, a retired butcher who had lived on his own since his wife's death. Ernie Bell just nodded briefly, eyeing the coach and its driver suspiciously. He was more difficult to get along with than Walter, though Mandy knew that his grumpy manner hid a kind heart.

"We didn't know you were interested in the big city, Mr. Pickard," James said to Walter, but it was Ernie who replied.

"Think we're too old for it, do you?" he growled, reluctantly letting Bill take his suitcase and wedge it on top of Miss Davy's neat zip-up bag. "You're as bad as that Ponsonby woman. Don't *you* start going on about too much excitement being dangerous at our time of life. She's not the only one who can go gadding off down south, you know!"

Mandy tried hard not to smile. She couldn't think of anything more certain to send Ernie off to London than Mrs. Ponsonby telling him he shouldn't go. Mrs. Ponsonby was always bossing everyone around and giving them advice they didn't want to hear. She wasn't so good at taking advice herself, though. Mandy often told her that Pandora, her fat Pekingese, needed less food and more exercise, but it was no good. Mrs. Ponsonby still gave Pandora tidbits and carried her everywhere. Things had only improved a little since she'd taken in a mongrel puppy, Toby, who encouraged Pandora to run around and play like a normal dog.

Lately, Mrs. Ponsonby had been more annoying than ever. She'd been invited to a garden party at Buckingham Palace because of all her work for charity. Everyone in the village had heard about it at least twenty times. Somehow, over the last few weeks, Mrs. Ponsonby had managed to get the words, "When I'm in London" and "When I meet the Queen" into every conversation. The garden party coincided with the Women's Club trip, but much to everyone's relief, Mrs. Ponsonby had decided to drive herself to the city rather than traveling by bus with the rest of them.

"We knew there were a few spare places on the trip." Walter explained quietly to Mandy and James, "but we didn't really think it was for us. And then Mrs. Ponsonby told Ernie that she understood why he didn't want to go. London was no place for an old fellow like him, set in his ways. So we decided to come after all." He gave them a wink.

"That's great!" said Mandy, starting to climb into the minibus. "I'm glad you did." Then a thought suddenly occurred to her, and she whirled around, nearly sending James flying. "But who's going to look after Missie and Scraps and Tom?" Walter had three cats, and then there was Ernie's cat, Twinkie, to consider, too, not to mention his pet squirrel, Sammy.

"Don't worry," Walter reassured her. "We wouldn't leave and abandon them. That young boy from the pub is stopping by twice a day to feed them, and he's in charge of Twinkie and Sammy, too. He came around yesterday, and we showed him where everything is."

"Of course! John's back now, isn't he?" Mandy remembered.

John Hardy was the son of Julian Hardy, the landlord of the Fox and Goose, and he came back to Welford from boarding school every vacation. Living so close by, he was the ideal person to look after Walter's and Ernie's pets.

"John's certainly going to be busy," Miss Davy said briskly. "He's feeding my hens as well and shutting them up for the night. I hope he's going to take his duties seriously."

Right on cue, an upstairs window in the pub flew open, and John Hardy's tousled head emerged. As he waved to them, Mandy felt a twinge of jealousy. She'd have loved being in charge of all those animals! A fresh surge of excitement soon stopped her from feeling too envious, though.

When everyone was finally on board, Bill checked his watch again and they were off. The minibus pulled slowly out of the parking lot and started down the road on its long trip to London.

They had only driven a short distance when Bill suddenly gave a shout of alarm and slammed on the brakes so sharply that all the passengers were thrown forward. The book Miss Davy had just opened flew across the aisle, James lost his headphones, and Mrs. McFarlane nearly choked on her peppermint.

James leaned around the seats in front to look through the windshield, then nudged Mandy without speaking. He pointed up ahead, and she followed his glance. In the middle of the road stood none other than

Mrs. Ponsonby herself, puffing and panting and red in the face. She had a large suitcase and a hatbox at her feet. Her Peke, Pandora, was tucked under one arm, and she was waving the minibus down with the other.

"Stop this bus!" she shouted loudly.

Two

"Really, driver!" Mrs. Ponsonby said severely after Bill had opened the minibus door. "What kind of speed is that for a narrow country road? You nearly ran me down! Now, please take my luggage, but do be careful. The hat in this box is an original design."

Bill gave her a long look as though deciding whether to reply and then shook his head. Glancing at his watch, he grumbled, "No time to open the trunk. You'll have to keep your bag with you." He yanked up the suitcase and stowed it between the seats. Mrs. Ponsonby clucked her tongue in annoyance, then picked up her hatbox, clutched Pandora more firmly, and prepared to climb on board.

"Grandma! You didn't tell us Mrs. Ponsonby was coming," Mandy hissed through to the seats in front, where her grandmother was sitting on her own.

"I didn't know she was!" came Dorothy Hope's horrified reply.

"Here — you can't bring that animal onto my minibus!" Bill told Mrs. Ponsonby, having just noticed Pandora. "What if it makes a mess on the floor?"

"Pandora is not just an 'animal,' she is a pedigree Pekingese," Mrs. Ponsonby announced grandly. "And she will not make a mess on the floor, I can assure you." She pushed past him indignantly and sank into the empty seat next to Dorothy Hope.

Bill shook his head again. "You'd better be right," he muttered doubtfully, starting the engine and preparing to drive off.

"Poor Grandma!" Mandy whispered to James, making a sympathetic face. She knew Mrs. Ponsonby really got on her grandmother's nerves. Now she would have to sit beside her all the way to London, with no chance of escape.

"I thought Mrs. Ponsonby was driving down later," James whispered back. "What's she doing here now?"

Together they listened as Mrs. Ponsonby explained to Dorothy Hope. "I decided to take the doggies out for a little drive last night, but — would you believe it — the car just wouldn't start! And who knows if I could have gotten it fixed in time to drive to London on Monday. One simply can't take any risks when one is meeting the Queen!" She laughed and patted her hat while Mrs. Hope murmured something Mandy couldn't hear.

"Anyway," Mrs. Ponsonby went on, "I remembered there were some spare places on your little expedition. By that time it was too late to phone you and check, and I must have just missed you when I called this morning. So Pandora and I set off to meet you on the road! How lucky there's an empty seat next to you, Dorothy. We can chat all the way."

"Very lucky," Mandy's grandma echoed faintly.

"But where's Toby, Mrs. Ponsonby?" Mandy asked, undoing her seat belt for a few seconds and leaning over the top of the seats to give Pandora a quick pat.

"Oh, I've left him with my sister," she replied, turning around to smile graciously at Mandy. "Toby is a delightful creature, of course, but he might be a little — shall we say — unpredictable, staying in a hotel. Not to mention at Buckingham Palace! I'm afraid the excitement would be too much for him. He might forget himself."

Mandy caught James's eye, and they both collapsed

into giggles behind the seat backs at the thought of Toby forgetting himself during a garden party at Buckingham Palace.

"What about your hotel?" Mandy's grandma asked Mrs. Ponsonby, as though an alarming thought had just occurred to her. "Can they fit you in over the weekend? I'm afraid our bed-and-breakfast is fully booked. Walter and Ernie have to stay in a pub around the corner."

"Don't worry about that, my dear," came the reply. "I phoned the hotel last night and they can squeeze us in for a few extra nights. After all, I don't really think a bed-and-breakfast is quite our sort of place, is it, Pandora? And as for a pub . . ." She shuddered.

"Well, I think it's great here," Mandy said, bouncing on the bed in the twin room she was sharing with her grandmother. "Good choice, Grandma!"

The Welford group was staying in small hotels, pubs, or guest houses in Greenwich, not far from the Millennium Dome. Dorothy Hope had booked her family and friends into a large Victorian house called the Crow's Nest on one of the narrow streets near the river. Mandy had held her breath as Bill steered the minibus expertly through the traffic. There were so many cars and so many people! It was all very different from the quiet green fields and country roads of Welford.

"There you are," Bill said as he parked opposite the guest house and checked his watch again. "Five to two. By the time I've unloaded all your luggage, it'll be two o'clock precisely!"

Inside the Crow's Nest everything was orderly and calm. The place was run by a fair-haired Scotsman with a bristly reddish beard who introduced himself as "Alexander McPherson, though everyone calls me Mac." He showed them all to their rooms before starting to take their luggage upstairs. Mandy's parents had a double room with a four-poster bed that they were delighted with. Eileen Davy and Mrs. McFarlane were sharing a room, while James was on his own next door to Mandy and her grandmother. Mrs. Platt was staying with her son over in Wimbledon, though she was going to meet up with the others for their trip to the Millennium Dome.

"If you don't mind, dear," Dorothy said, sitting on the other bed, "I think I'll have a nap now. Six hours of Mrs. Ponsonby has nearly finished me off. Why don't you and James go exploring?"

"Okay, Grandma," Mandy said. "I can understand just how you feel!"

She shut the door quietly behind her and went next door to get James. Just like the bedrooms, the walls of the corridor were hung with old maps and prints of sailing ships.

James's room was full of model boats, too. "I bet Mac's been a sailor at one time or another," Mandy commented, picking up an ornament on the chest of drawers. It was a bottle, with a tiny ship sailing along inside it. "How on earth did that get in there?" she wondered, fascinated.

James shrugged. "Well, he certainly loves the sea," he said, laying his books on the bedside table. "Did you see the ship's wheel at the top of the stairs?"

Mandy nodded. "Let's go and explore when you've finished unpacking," she said, putting down the bottle. After hours of sitting still on the bus, she felt like stretching her legs.

A few minutes later, they walked along the landing, past the huge oak wheel, and down the staircase. James paused to look at a large print hanging at the bottom of the stairs. "So that's what Greenwich was like three hundred years ago," he said to Mandy, reading the caption beneath the picture. "Look at all those ships on the Thames!"

"Aye, the river was a busy old place," said Mac, who was just about to take the last of the suitcases upstairs. "There's been many a king and queen of England who'd sail upriver to Greenwich and bring the whole court with them, too. Henry VIII was born here, you know, and Elizabeth I used to spend the summers at Greenwich."

Mandy glanced around the crowded hall. There were so many things to look at! Wooden seagulls, which were suspended from the ceiling, flapped their wings gracefully when she and James pulled their cords. In one corner stood a big ironbound chest, and above it were shelves crammed with what looked like old navigational instruments — a brass telescope, a compass, and others Mandy couldn't identify. Shells and crystals were on display, too, and a huge shark's jawbone. Mac put down the luggage he was carrying and came over to the two friends when he noticed them looking at it.

"Did you know that a shark's teeth are arranged in rows?" he said, taking the jawbone off the shelf to show it to them. "So if the creature loses a tooth, another grows forward from behind to take its place."

Mandy shivered, examining the sharp, jagged teeth. "They're vicious!" she said.

"Absolutely right." Mac smiled, picking up the bags and setting off upstairs again. "Once a shark gets ahold of you, you won't get away in a hurry."

Mandy was examining a bundle of wooden walking sticks carved with animal heads when all of a sudden she heard a squeaky little meow. "Did you hear that?" she asked James, looking eagerly all around. "I think there's a cat here somewhere!" A real animal rather than a carved or painted one would make the Crow's Nest just perfect as far as she was concerned.

"There it is!" James said quietly, nudging Mandy and pointing toward a large globe in another corner. Peeping shyly out from behind it was a small tortoiseshell cat. Its tawny fur was striped with ginger, brown, and black, and its large golden eyes were as round as saucers.

"I thought so!" Mandy said, dropping to her knees and smiling at the cat. She held out her hand and called in a soft, encouraging voice, "Come on, kitty! Come and say hello."

The tortoiseshell gave another little meow and ventured out from behind the globe. Mandy scratched on the rug with her fingers, and the cat bounded over, pouncing on her hand and batting it with soft paws.

"Oh, isn't she lovely!" Mandy said, grinning up at James as she played with the little creature.

"How do you know it's a she?" James asked, crouching down beside Mandy.

"Tortoiseshells are nearly always female," Mandy said, hoping she didn't sound too much like a know-it-all. "We had a male tortoiseshell in the clinic the other day with fur balls, but Dad told me they are really rare." She scratched the cat below her ears, and the animal began to purr, pushing her head into Mandy's hand as she petted the soft, thick fur. Then, with a wave of her tail, the cat wandered across the hall to a half-open door. Looking back at them, she meowed again.

"Looks like she wants us to follow her," Mandy said, getting to her feet. "Perhaps we're going to get a guided tour!"

She went after the cat into what looked like a dining room, full of tables and chairs. The little tortoiseshell dived under one of the tables and began to play with the trailing edge of the tablecloth, rolling onto her back again and clutching the fabric fiercely with sharp claws.

"Careful!" Mandy said, disentangling the cloth. "You'll tear it, and then Mac won't be pleased."

"Look at that, Mandy!" James said behind her, and she followed his pointing finger. Mounted on the opposite wall was a huge, painted, wooden bust of a woman. She was staring into the distance with large, unseeing eyes, and long dark hair streamed out behind her as though blown by some invisible wind. The name DAISY MAY was painted in flowing golden script on the blue shawl draped around her neck.

"Wow! That must be an old ship's figurehead," Mandy said, awestruck. "It looks like she's bursting through the wall and heading straight for us. Spooky, isn't it?"

But before James could reply, there was a sudden explosion of noise. A loud, harsh voice came ringing through the air. "Good-bye!" it shouted menacingly. "Time to go!"

"What's that?" James shouted, grabbing Mandy's arm. "Who's there?"

"I don't know," she replied desperately, searching the room for some sign of whoever — or whatever — was screaming at them. The voice rang out again, even louder this time. Desperate to block out the terrifying noise, Mandy clamped her hands over her ears. But it was no good.

"Everybody's gone home!" it shrieked this time. "Time for bed! Night-night, sleep tight!"

The tortoiseshell cat streaked out of the room, leaving Mandy and James alone with what sounded like a madman.

"Come on, James!" Mandy cried. "We've got to get out of here!"

Three

"Look behind you!" screamed the invisible voice. Mandy and James whirled around, but there was nobody there.

"Who's that?" Mandy called as bravely as she could, beginning to feel angry now as well as frightened. Somebody seemed to be playing a joke at their expense, and it wasn't very funny.

"Daisy May is a wicked woman," the voice said in a lower, plaintive tone.

"Wh-where are you?" James cried uncertainly. "Come out and show yourself!"

"Have a nice day," the voice mocked, and then cackled. Mandy and James heard another peal of laughter behind them. They turned around to see a tall girl of about their age, with shoulder-length brown hair, watching them from the doorway with an amused look on her face.

"What's going on?" Mandy demanded, feeling slightly stupid and loosening James's grip on her arm.

"Looks like you've just met Sinbad for the first time," the girl replied. She walked into the room and pointed toward a dark corner. There in the shadows stood a big cage on wheels. Inside it, a gray bird was walking delicately along the thick tree branch that served as a perch.

"So he was the one making all that noise?" Mandy said, scarcely able to believe her eyes. Her heart was still thumping madly, and her palms prickled with sweat. "Do you mean we've just been frightened half to death by a *parrot*?"

She and James went up to the birdcage for a closer look. Sinbad was slate gray, apart from his scarlet tail and the silvery-white mask around his small yellow eyes. The feathers on his neck were edged in a paler shade, so that each one looked distinct and separate. Mandy thought he was just as beautiful as some of the more brightly colored birds she'd seen.

"Hello, Sinbad," she said cautiously, but the parrot seemed to have decided he'd done enough talking. He stared silently at her and then sank his head down between his shoulders, ruffling up the feathers.

"He's not very friendly, is he?" James said to the girl, who'd come up to the cage beside them. "Doesn't he like meeting strangers?"

"I asked Mac about him yesterday, when we arrived," she replied. "He said Sinbad's feeling very grumpy at the moment for some reason, and it's best not to pay him too much attention. My name's Casey Baxter, by the way. I'm on vacation over here, from New York."

James and Mandy introduced themselves, too, and then Mandy turned back to the parrot in his cage. She couldn't help wondering why Sinbad was so hostile. "He's a great talker," she said to Casey. "I wonder if we can teach him anything more friendly to say."

"Something tells me he's not in a very friendly mood," Casey replied.

They watched as Sinbad made his way over to the container of seeds at the side of his cage and picked up a peanut with his foot. He cracked the shell with his strong curved beak and used his tongue to help take out the nut inside. James whistled the parrot a tune, but Sinbad only glared at him suspiciously.

"Let's let him sulk for the moment," Casey said to them. "Have you seen the garden yet? Come on, I'll show you."

They said good-bye to Sinbad and left him in the quiet dining room. "We'll come to see you again soon," Mandy promised, thinking the parrot looked rather forlorn as they left. She made up her mind to ask Mac all about him.

"This is such a cool place," Casey told them as they went along a corridor to the back door. "My dad's a doctor, and someone who works at the hospital with him visited London last year. He told us we just had to stay here."

"Do you know why the house is so full of boats and sailing things?" Mandy asked.

"Oh, that's because Mac used to be a ship's cook," Casey replied, opening the door to a small courtyard garden at the back of the house. "Just wait till you see breakfast tomorrow!" she added, walking down a cobbled path to a blue-painted bench. "You won't need to eat again for the rest of the day, I'm telling you."

"Have you had a look around Greenwich yet?" asked James, sitting down beside her.

"Yes, I have," Casey said. "We got up early this morning. There's so much to see! The park, and the Observatory, and a couple of palaces, and this wonderful ship called the *Cutty Sark*. It's amazing — full of figureheads like old Daisy May in the dining room. Hey, maybe I could show it to you this afternoon! And then tomorrow we're going to see the changing of the guard at Buckingham Palace. You'll have to come with us — if you'd like to, that is. We're going to Madame Tussaud's in the afternoon, but you have to reserve tickets, otherwise you'll be in line for a year, Mom says."

"Slow down," Mandy laughed. "You're making me feel tired!" She gazed around the garden. To her delight, there was the tortoiseshell cat, lying in a sunny spot beneath a rosemary bush. She walked over to say hello. The cat got to her feet, arched her back, and then twined around Mandy's legs, meowing.

"That's Patch," Casey called over. "She's beautiful, isn't she?"

"Lovely!" Mandy replied, picking Patch up and burying her face in the cat's soft, warm fur. She suddenly felt quite certain that they couldn't have found a nicer place to stay in all of London.

The next day it was time to start sight-seeing. The Hopes met Casey's parents over a huge breakfast that morning, and they were soon getting along so well they decided to spend the day together.

"That's awesome!" Casey said to Mandy a few hours later as they gazed between tall iron railings at the imposing sight of Buckingham Palace stretched out in front of them. "So this is where the Queen lives when she's in London, right? Do you think she's looking down on us at this very moment?"

"She might be," James said. He pointed to a red-and-gold flag fluttering against the blue sky. "Look, the Royal Standard's flying. When she's not at the Palace, they put up the Union Jack instead. I was reading all about it in my guidebook last night."

"Wow!" Casey grinned. She waved her arm toward the empty balcony. "How d'you do, Your Majesty? This is Casey Baxter from New York, just dropping by to say hello!"

Mandy turned to watch all the people around them. Tour guides held up different colored umbrellas so they could be seen by their groups, families posed for photographs, and hot-dog sellers jostled for the best position. Mandy wrinkled her nose. The frying onions smelled delicious, but as a vegetarian, she wasn't tempted by the sausages.

All of a sudden, she spotted something she hadn't expected to see. Sitting near one of the hot-dog stands was an adorable chocolate-brown Labrador puppy, head cocked to one side as it stared longingly up at the sausages. Mandy looked at the pup more closely and then at the people standing around it. No one seemed to be taking much notice of the little dog, but she felt sure its owner was somewhere nearby. An animal as young as that wouldn't have been left to wander around alone in the middle of London.

Casey was still engrossed in what was happening at the Palace, so Mandy nudged James. "Look!" she said. "There's a puppy over there, and it seems to be all on its own. Do you think it's run away from someone?"

"Oh, isn't it cute?" James said as he spotted the little pup. "You're right, though — there doesn't seem to be anybody looking after it. Is it wearing a collar?"

"I'm not sure," Mandy said, narrowing her eyes as she stared. "We're too far away to tell. Come on, let's go a bit nearer and find out what's happening."

"Where are you going? You'll lose your place!" Casey called after them from her lookout post by the railings, but James and Mandy were already hurrying away.

"We'll be back in a second," Mandy called over her shoulder. There was no time to explain.

"I think I've got something that might help us catch the puppy if we need to," James said, searching his jacket pockets as they threaded their way through the crowd. "Yes! Here it is!" Triumphantly, he pulled out an ancient-looking dog biscuit. "Left over from one of Blackie's obedience classes," he explained.

"Great!" Mandy said, her eyes fixed on the puppy. Some people in the crowd were glancing at it from time to time and smiling, but most of them were too busy waiting for something to happen at the Palace to pay much attention to the pup.

"It's not trailing a leash," James said as they approached. "I don't even think it's wearing a collar."

"And it's definitely alone," Mandy added. "We'd better try to catch it, in case it takes off into the traffic." She crouched down a little way off, not wanting to frighten the young animal away, and clapped her hands on her thighs to attract its attention. "Come on," she called cheerfully. "There's a good dog! Look what we've got for you!"

The pup looked up at the sound of her voice and raised its soft brown ears inquiringly. "That's the way!" James called encouragingly, holding out the dog biscuit. "Over here!"

The puppy gave a short bark and bounded toward them, ears pricked and tail wagging furiously at the sight — and smell — of food. "You're hungry, aren't you?" Mandy said as she watched it wolf down the biscuit James was offering.

"Labrador puppies are always hungry," James said, smiling, as the pup licked his hand with a rough pink tongue. "Do you remember what Blackie was like when he was small? He'd eat anything in sight! And this puppy looks like it's smiling at us, just like Blackie does. Do you think it's male or female?"

"Hard to tell for sure," Mandy replied as she watched the puppy frisking around. "It won't keep still for long enough, but I think it's a male dog, don't you? Mom and Dad can tell us if I'm right."

The young dog had lost his fat baby stomach, but he still had that soft, puppyish look around the face and seemed not quite able to control his long legs yet. Mandy patted his silky brown fur, and the pup pushed a damp, cold nose into her hand.

"He doesn't look like a stray," James said. "His coat's in fantastic condition."

Mandy petted one of the puppy's soft ears, and he gazed adoringly up at her with melting brown eyes. "No, I think you've got a good home somewhere, don't you?" she asked. "And we've got to get you back there!"

The puppy gave another short bark and began to dash around them, wagging his tail furiously and crouching down on his front legs, waiting for James and Mandy to join in the game.

"Quick, James!" Mandy cried, unbuckling the belt around her jeans so she could use it as a temporary leash. "We have to catch him before he runs off again!"

"Let me just get a photo," James said, already looking through the viewfinder of his camera. The puppy stared inquisitively back at him.

And then disaster struck. A mounted policewoman

on a dapple-gray horse rode up to the hot-dog sellers. "Clear this area immediately!" she said in a loud voice. "You've been told a hundred times not to operate here. It's illegal. Go on, get going — right now. There are horses coming, and you'd better not get in the way!"

At once, everyone in the crowd surged forward, cameras at the ready, to get a good look at the Household Cavalry who were riding down past Buckingham Palace on the way back to their barracks in Hyde Park. Grumbling, the hot-dog sellers began to wheel their trolleys away through the throng. But in all the chaos, the puppy disappeared.

"Where is he?" Mandy cried desperately, looking around. Normally, she'd have loved to watch the mounted guards riding past on their sleek, beautifully groomed black horses. But now all she could think about was the little animal. She hated to think of him being trampled under the horses' hooves or running out into the road and getting knocked over by a car. "James, we have to find the puppy quickly!"

"I can't see him anywhere!" he shouted back, already separated from Mandy by a crowd of people. "He seems to have vanished!"

Frantically, they looked down and searched through the forest of legs around them for any sign of the pup.

But it was hopeless — there was no trace of the little dog.

"Let's go and find Mom and Dad," Mandy called to James. "They can help us search. Come on, there's no time to lose!"

"I don't think there's anything more we can do for now," Dr. Emily said, putting a comforting arm around Mandy's shoulders. "I don't want you and James getting lost in the crowd as well — that won't help anybody. Let's wait until it starts to thin out, and then we'll be able to spot this puppy of yours. Why don't you go and watch with Casey for a while?"

"Okay," Mandy said disconsolately. "I suppose it might take our mind off things. We'll see you back here when the changing of the guard is finished."

It took James and Mandy a while to make their way through the packed crowd of tourists. Eventually, though, they spotted Casey's baseball cap and managed to join her by the railings at the front, where the best views were.

"What happened to you two?" she asked.

"We spotted this little lost puppy by a hot-dog stand," Mandy explained miserably, "but he ran away before we could catch him."

"Oh, no!" Casey said, giving Mandy a sympathetic pat on the back. "When the display is over, I'll help you search some more. Look, here come the new guards!"

A group of soldiers in scarlet-and-black uniforms had appeared on the Palace forecourt and were marching toward the sentry boxes. Mandy was more interested in looking at the wide pavement behind her, though, just in case she spotted a flash of brown fur or a waving tail.

Suddenly, Casey grabbed her arm. "That puppy!" she

asked excitedly. "It wasn't a chocolate-brown Lab, by any chance, was it?"

"Yes, it was!" Mandy replied eagerly. "Why? Have you seen him?"

"Looks like he's just joined up for guard duty," Casey grinned. "Here, pull yourself up next to me so you can watch."

Mandy hoisted herself up by the railings and peered through. "I don't believe it!" she exclaimed. A few paces behind the guards was their missing puppy, walking along proudly, his tail held high.

"He must have slipped through the railings," James said, climbing up beside the two girls.

All around them, people had begun laughing and pointing at the puppy, talking excitedly in what sounded like twenty different languages. The guards didn't seem to notice that they had a new recruit, and the pup was careful to keep a few paces behind them. When they reached the first sentry box, the little dog quickly nipped behind it. For a few seconds there was nothing to be seen, but then a mischievous brown head peeked around the corner. The soldiers were so intent on changing the guard that none of them spotted it. Everyone else had, though, and a loud gale of laughter rose in the air.

"Naughty little thing!" Mandy smiled. "He obviously thinks it's a wonderful game."

Excited by the noise, the puppy decided he had had enough of marching and began to twirl around, chasing his tail. Then he bounded off through an archway that led to a courtyard within the Palace, and he disappeared from sight. There was a loud round of applause from the crowd.

"Well," said James, chuckling. "At least now we know he's safely away from the road."

"I suppose so," Mandy said doubtfully. "I just hope he'll be okay in there." She stared up at the long rows of windows, imagining the vast number of rooms inside the Palace, and frowned. The little dog might have found his way in, but would he ever manage to find a way out again?

Four

The next morning, Mandy was the first person down to the dining room. Mac was apparently in the middle of setting the breakfast tables, but he had stopped for a moment by the birdcage.

"Morning!" Mandy said, going over to join him. "How's Sinbad today?"

"He's calmed down a bit since yesterday," said Mac, turning away and starting to put out the cereal bowls. "I'm sorry he frightened you. Casey told me about it last night."

"That's okay," Mandy replied, watching Sinbad flex his

39

long toes and walk delicately along the wooden perch. "I think his voice is wonderful. I've never heard anything like it!"

"I wish all my guests agreed with you," Mac told her with a smile. "Sinbad's an amazing mimic, like lots of African grays, but some people don't find him very funny."

"I bet they don't," Mandy said. She could just imagine what Mrs. Ponsonby would say if Sinbad imitated her! The parrot cocked his head coyly and looked sideways at her out of one yellow eye. "He does seem happier today," she continued, watching as Sinbad began to preen his soft gray feathers carefully. "Do you think he'd let me take him out of the cage?"

"A couple of months ago, I'd have said yes right away." Mac sighed, folding a napkin. "But now I think it would be better not to risk it. He might take a swipe at you, and that beak is very sharp!" He finished with the pile of linens and then took some grapes from a bowl on the sideboard. "Here, why don't I take him out, and you can give him some fruit?" he suggested. "If you'd like to, that is. You seem very interested in him."

"Oh, I am!" Mandy replied. "My parents are vets, and that's what I'd like to be, too, if I can get the right grades. I've never met an African gray before."

"They're very intelligent birds," Mac said, passing her

the grapes and opening the cage door. "They can be nervous, but I've had Sinbad since he was a chick and tamed him myself." He stretched his hand into the cage, and Sinbad hopped onto his finger, chirping and whistling excitedly.

"I think he's beautiful," Mandy said, enjoying a good look at Sinbad out in the open. He watched Mac, turning his head this way and that, and seemed to listen intently as his owner talked to him. "He has so many different expressions, doesn't he?" Mandy said, offering the parrot a grape. "Like he's thinking all the time."

"You're right," Mac agreed. "And you should see him when he's about to sing! He ruffles up his neck feathers and looks very grand, like he's a famous Italian tenor!" They both laughed, and they watched as Sinbad carefully took the grape with one claw and raised it to his beak to nibble. "He doesn't sing much these days, though," Mac added quietly.

"Do you know why he's so miserable at the moment?" Mandy asked. She couldn't hear about an unhappy animal without wanting to help.

Mac shook his head. "I don't know what's gotten into him," he said anxiously. "I've taken him to the vet for a checkup, but there isn't anything physically wrong. He just doesn't seem himself at all — he's so moody! He doesn't talk half as much as he used to, and when he does, he can be very aggressive, like he was with you yesterday. But the worst thing is, he's started pulling out his feathers. Look there."

"Oh, yes, I see!" Mandy said. Several of the overlapping dark gray feathers on Sinbad's breast were missing, revealing the fluffy white down beneath. "Why would he do that?" she asked.

Mac frowned. "I have no idea," he answered, putting Sinbad carefully back into the cage and shutting the door. "I make sure he doesn't have mites, and I spray him with water so his skin doesn't get too dry. I wish he'd stop, though. The vet told me it's a habit that can quickly get out of control. Some birds pluck their skin bare."

"Oh, how horrible!" Mandy exclaimed. It was awful to think of Sinbad deliberately hurting himself. He obviously had lots of love and attention, so why should he need to do such a thing? "I'll ask Mom and Dad if there's anything we can do," she told Mac. "I'm sure they'll come up with something."

Mandy didn't get a chance to talk to her mother about Sinbad until later that morning when they were sitting on a boat together, sailing down the Thames. Mandy's grandma had suggested at breakfast that a trip down the river from Greenwich to Westminster would be a good way to see the sights. It was a lovely sunny morning, and everyone thought going out on the water was a wonderful idea. Walter and Ernie had met them at Greenwich Pier, which was just around the corner from the pub where they were staying, and Casey and her parents had come along, too. Dr. and Mrs. Baxter were getting along so well with the Hopes that it seemed natural for them all to go sight-seeing together again.

Dr. Emily was not very encouraging about Sinbad's prospects. "Feather plucking can turn into a serious problem very quickly," she said gravely. "There could be any number of explanations. Sinbad's skin might be irritated, or he might be under some kind of stress, or bored, or even ready for a mate. I'd be happy to have a look at him, but often there's no physical reason for that kind of behavior. You have to get to know the bird to find out why he's doing it."

"Well, then, maybe that's what we should do," James said. Mandy had told him all about Sinbad's problem, and he'd been listening in on the conversation with her mom. "Between us, we should be able to help him before we have to go back home."

"I don't know," Dr. Emily said, smiling at them both. "First puppies, now parrots! I thought we'd left all our patients back in Welford! Just don't let worrying about Sinbad spoil your vacation."

"We'll try not to," Mandy promised. If there was an animal somewhere in need of help, though, she and James wouldn't rest until they'd found a solution. And Mandy's mother was just the same, no matter what she might say.

"Look — straight ahead!" James said suddenly, focusing his binoculars on the river. "That was a cormorant, wasn't it?"

"You're right," Dr. Adam said from his seat a little farther up the boat. "There's another one sitting on that post over there. See how it holds its wings outstretched to dry them?"

"Here, look through these for a minute," James said to Mandy, passing her the binoculars.

"Thanks, James," Mandy replied, peering through them at the dark bird zigzagging down the river in front of them. Suddenly, it dipped down to the water and flew back up with a flash of silver in its beak. "Oh, it's caught something!" she exclaimed, handing the binoculars to Casey so she could see, too.

"There's all kinds of fish coming back to the Thames now that the water's so much cleaner," the riverboat captain told them, leaning out of his cabin. "You can even catch a salmon if you're lucky."

The recorded commentary crackled to life to tell everyone the boat was approaching Tower Bridge and that the Tower of London would soon be in full view on their right. They should look out for Traitors' Gate, where condemned prisoners were brought to the Tower by boat from the courts at Westminster. This would have been the last glimpse of the outside world for most of them.

"I can't wait to look around the Tower," Casey said as they sailed past the grim, forbidding building. "That's where the crown jewels are, right? And the execution block where they beheaded one of Henry VIII's wives?"

Mandy shivered. It all sounded very gloomy to her. As far as she was concerned, it was much more fun to be out in the sunshine on the river.

"That's right. We're going down as far as Westminster Pier now, but we can stop off on the way back," Dr. Adam promised, "after we've taken a look at Big Ben and Westminster Abbey. And maybe had a quick pizza," he added hopefully.

"Dad!" Mandy said, outraged. "On top of that huge breakfast? You'll have to go back on a diet when this trip's over!"

"I've never eaten a pizza in my life, and I don't intend to start now," Ernie declared. "A sandwich in the park will suit Walter and me, thank you very much. There was a brass band playing there yesterday at lunchtime. Not as good as some I've heard up north, mind you."

"But think what Mrs. Ponsonby would say if she heard you'd had pizza for lunch!" James said innocently. "She couldn't call you set in your ways then, could she, Mr. Bell?" He caught Mandy's eye, and she had to bite her lip hard to stop herself from smiling.

Ernie thought for a while. "Maybe not," he said eventually. "I'll have to see how I feel."

"Speaking of Mrs. Ponsonby," Mandy's grandma broke in, "she called the Crow's Nest last night. I think she's lonely in that expensive hotel of hers. Anyway, she's invited us all to lunch tomorrow."

"But we're going to look around the Royal Mews tomorrow!" Mandy protested. "Dad promised he'd take us." On their way back from Buckingham Palace the day before, James had spotted a sign for the Royal Mews, the largest working stable in London. It was closed on weekends, but Mandy, James, and Casey all wanted to go back there on Monday. A chance to see the Queen's magnificent carriage horses close up was just too good to miss. And besides, they might be able to ask someone if a Labrador puppy had been found anywhere in the Palace. Mandy was counting on that!

"Don't worry," her grandmother reassured her. "I suggested we all meet for a picnic in St. James's Park. It's opposite the Palace, so you won't have to miss out on anything."

"And we can take Pandora for a walk," James said. "I bet Mrs. Ponsonby hasn't been exercising her properly."

"Oh, James, that's a great idea," Mandy said, beaming at him. "Who knows, we might even get Dad to go jogging!"

"Mom, Dad, after we've seen Westminster Abbey, do you think we could climb the tower in Westminster Cathedral?" Mandy asked, looking up from James's guide book. They were all standing beside Big Ben, waiting for James to finish photographing the clock face. "It's in Victoria Street, where the shops are," she went on, "so I'm sure there'll be a restaurant nearby."

"Well, okay, as long as the Baxters are happy with that," Dr. Adam replied. "I didn't realize you liked sightseeing so much, love."

On their way over to the cathedral, Mandy explained her plan to James and Casey. "According to James's book, you can see right into the gardens at Buckingham Palace from the top of the tower," she said as they walked along the empty Sunday-morning street. "I know it's a long shot, but if we can get a good view —"

"We might be able to spot that Labrador puppy we saw yesterday," James finished for her, slinging the binoculars around his neck.

"Exactly!" Mandy said. She knew that James wouldn't have forgotten the little dog, either. The puppy had probably been found by now, but there was a slim chance it might still be running around the Palace grounds. Perhaps if they spotted it, they could alert one of the police officers by the gate. At the very least, it would be good to see the pup again and make sure it was safe.

They soon reached the cathedral, set back from the road with a large paved area in front. Dr. Emily put her finger to her lips as they went through the huge doors because there was a church service going on. They made their way quietly to the elevator that would take them up to the viewing platform.

"Well, that's a real English elevator," Dr. Baxter said as its doors opened. "It's half the size of our elevators! We won't all fit in."

"Why don't I take the youngsters up first?" the attendant suggested. "It's safe up top — you can't fall over."

"Good idea!" Mandy said at once. She knew her mother felt she should stop worrying about animals and just enjoy the vacation, so it would be much better if they had a few minutes on their own to look for the pup.

The view from the top of the tower might have been

spectacular, but it was a big disappointment as far as they were concerned. "Maybe you could see into the Palace gardens ten years ago," James said, squinting through his binoculars, "but you certainly can't now. There's a great big office building in the way!"

Mandy sighed as she looked toward Buckingham Palace. She could just see the golden top of the Victoria monument outside its gates and the green trees in St. James's Park, but that was about it. There was no way they could look into the gardens, even with binoculars. And then, suddenly, a flurry of activity beneath them caught her eye. Some tourists were milling around in the square below while a small shape ran to and fro around their group. A small brown shape . . .

"James! Casey! Look down there, where those people are," she cried excitedly. "I think it might be the puppy!"

"Where?" Casey demanded, squeezing in beside her and peering down. "I can't see where you mean. Hang on a minute! Yes! You're right — that's him!"

"Looks like he's playing with somebody," James added. "Or maybe chasing a pigeon."

"Well, then, what are we waiting for? Come on, let's see if we can get him!" Mandy cried, already rushing out. "Quick, before he runs off again!"

Casey's parents and the Hopes were just getting out of the elevator as Mandy, James, and Casey arrived to take it back down. "We've had a good look," Mandy told her parents quickly as the three of them squeezed into the lift. "See you downstairs, outside the cathedral."

"What's going on?" Mrs. Baxter asked. "Why are you in such a hurry?"

"We'll explain later," Casey promised as the elevator doors closed and the surprised attendant started taking them back to ground level.

"Come on, elevator," Mandy groaned as they creaked slowly downward. "Hurry up! I couldn't bear it if we lost the puppy again. We're so close now!"

Eventually the doors opened. They walked through the quiet cathedral as quickly as they could without running, and then out into the square. "Oh, no!" James cried in dismay. "Where'd he go?" The tourists were scattering toward the street, and there was no sign of the little dog anywhere among them.

"We're looking for the puppy that was here a minute ago," Mandy said to a large man wearing sunglasses at the back of the group. "Did you see where he went?" But the man just smiled and waved at her, obviously not understanding a word.

"There he is!" Casey shouted suddenly. "Look, down that little street!" She rushed across the square and then stepped out to cross the side street — straight into the path of a black London taxi. There was a horrible squeal of brakes, followed by the even more terrifying noise of a heavy thud as Casey's body hit the front of the cab.

"Casey!" Mandy screamed, running toward her. "James, go back and get Dr. Baxter — and hurry!"

Five

Mandy flew across the sidewalk toward Casey, her heart pounding and her eyes fixed on the slumped body. Casey had been thrown back by the force of the collision and was now lying, terrifyingly still, on the sidewalk. As Mandy approached, though, she saw Casey begin to struggle up on one elbow.

"No! Stop!" she cried, kneeling beside her. "Just stay here — don't try to get up." She knew from experience with animals that had been run over that a patient shouldn't be moved before getting medical attention. That could do further damage to broken bones or back injuries.

The taxi driver came rushing over to join them, his face as pale as Casey's. "Is she all right?" he asked desperately. "Tell me she's not badly hurt!"

"I don't think so," Mandy said, quickly taking off her jacket and folding it into a pillow that she tucked under Casey's head. Casey was as white as a sheet and trembling a little, but her breathing was regular and her skin wasn't cold and clammy. As far as Mandy could tell, she wasn't in serious shock.

"What happened?" she asked in a dazed voice.

"You had an argument with a London taxi," Mandy said as calmly as she could, smoothing the hair back from Casey's face. "I think the taxi won. Just lie still for now. Everything's going to be fine. Don't worry."

"Why won't you let me get up off the sidewalk?" Casey asked feebly. "I feel like an idiot lying here." A small crowd was gathering around them by now. People were craning curiously to see who had been knocked over and if the victim was badly hurt.

"I think we should wait till your parents arrive," Mandy said, pushing up the sleeve of Casey's sweatshirt so she could check that her pulse wasn't racing too fast. "James has gone to get them, so your dad'll be here any minute. He's a doctor," she added for the taxi driver's benefit.

"Well, I can see she's in good hands," he replied thankfully, wiping a shaking hand across his forehead. "Thanks. There was nothing I could do! She just stepped out in front of me!"

By now the Baxters were racing toward them, with James and the Hopes not far behind. Dr. Baxter pushed his way through to Casey, then crouched down and began running his hands expertly over her body, talking to her all the while in a calm, gentle voice. Casey's mom knelt at her daughter's head, stroking her hair and trying very hard not to cry.

Quietly, Mandy stepped away. She'd done all she could, and she felt the Baxters needed some privacy. Her father obviously agreed. He began to clear all the onlookers away. In a firm but pleasant voice, he asked everyone to give the family some space, telling them that everything was under control.

"Well done, love," Mandy's mom said, giving her a comforting hug. "Looks like you've done exactly the right thing."

"Do you think she'll be okay?" James asked anxiously. Mandy nodded, not trusting herself to speak. She'd been fine when there was something to do, but now the shock of the accident was beginning to hit her. And then she remembered why Casey had been rushing across the street in the first place. The puppy! She looked toward the side street, but it seemed deserted.

James followed her gaze. "I'll go and take a quick look," he said quietly. "As long as there's nothing else I can do —"

"I think Casey's parents are the best people to look after her now," Mandy said. "Thanks, James."

At last Dr. Baxter began to help Casey up. "She's fine, amazingly enough," he said when Casey was back on her feet, looking rather unsteady. "No broken bones, and no internal injuries, either — just a big shock to the system."

Mandy let out her breath in relief, and everyone broke into smiles.

"Thank God!" said the taxi driver. "I'm so sorry! She stepped right out in front of me," he repeated to Casey's parents. "Maybe she's not used to the traffic?"

"Hey! I live in New York," Casey told him in a shaky voice. "Of course I'm used to traffic! I'm just not used to it coming at me from the wrong direction, that's all."

"We're going to get a nice hot cup of English tea and then go straight back to Greenwich," said Mrs. Baxter, blowing her nose on a tissue. "I think we've had enough excitement for one day."

"I'll catch you later," Casey said to Mandy as she was led away. "We'll have a talk about you know what!"

Just then, Mandy saw James hurrying back toward her. She raised her eyebrows at him in a silent question although she could already tell from his disappointed expression that he had nothing to report. He just shook his head.

"And now I think *we* need a little chat, don't you?" Mandy's mother asked them both sternly. "What were the three of you up to? Why was Casey running across the street like that?"

Mandy and James looked at each other and then down at the ground. "We spotted the puppy again when we were up in the tower," Mandy said eventually. "Casey saw it go down that side street, but now it's run off somewhere else."

Dr. Emily sighed. "Didn't you remember what I told you this morning?" she asked Mandy, a serious look in her green eyes. "Look, of course we have to help an animal in trouble, but this puppy search seems to be turning into a wild-goose chase — and a dangerous one at that. Casey could have been killed just now!"

"London is a huge place," Dr. Adam added firmly. "We can't possibly spend our whole vacation searching for a puppy that could be anywhere by now. It'd be like looking for a needle in a haystack! Somebody will find him and take him to the police, I'm sure of it. So no more running around after lost dogs, okay? And certainly not now — it's time for lunch!"

"Okay," said Mandy, realizing that she had to accept what her parents said — for the time being, at least. Inside her head, though, she made the puppy a silent promise. *Don't worry, we won't forget about you. We'll keep looking, if we can!*

When Mandy, James, and her parents got back to the Crow's Nest later that afternoon, Mac told them that Casey was resting in her room. The next morning, when the Baxters came down to breakfast, Mandy noticed Casey was walking a little stiffly. "How are you?" she asked her right away. "We've been so worried!"

"Oh, I really am fine," Casey said. "Just feeling kind of stupid for causing all this fuss and bother. And I have a bruise on my back the size of a dinner plate." She sat down next to Mandy and James. "I don't suppose you saw any sign of the pup after all that commotion, did you?" she asked.

"No. I went down the side street to look, but he'd disappeared," James replied, unfolding his napkin.

Mandy took a quick glance at her parents, sitting at the next table, and saw they were already chatting away with Dr. and Mrs. Baxter. "Mom and Dad told us we should forget about the puppy for now," she told Casey, lowering her voice. "But I hate to think of him running around those busy streets. I wish he'd stayed in the Palace — he'd have been safer there."

"I'm sure someone will catch him soon," Casey said comfortingly, helping herself to orange juice from a big jug. "He can't stay on the loose forever."

"Just so long as he doesn't get knocked over first," Mandy worried, holding out her glass so Casey could fill it, too. "And what's he finding to eat? Where's he sleeping at night?"

"I bet he's found someone to look after him by now,"

James answered reassuringly as he started eating a bowl of cereal. "He's such a friendly little thing. Anyway, we'll be able to keep our eyes open for any sign of him when we go to the Royal Mews this morning. You are coming, aren't you, Casey?"

"'Fraid not," Casey said. "I'm still under house arrest. Dad says I've got to have a couple more quiet days before he'll let me back into the city."

So after breakfast they said good-bye to Casey and set off for the Royal Mews. Dorothy Hope, Mrs. McFarlane, and Eileen Davy were going to meet them at lunchtime in St. James's Park, bringing a picnic Mac had prepared. "Though I'm not sure a picnic will be grand enough for Mrs. Ponsonby," Mandy's grandmother told her. "After a weekend in that wonderful hotel of hers, she's probably not prepared to sit on a blanket in the park!"

Mandy stared up and down the street as she walked with James and her parents toward the Royal Mews at the side of Buckingham Palace. It was really close to where they'd been the day before — just a couple of streets away from Westminster Cathedral. But what busy streets they were! Mandy felt her heart sink as she watched the speeding traffic and the hundreds of people hurrying along the sidewalk. How could any puppy find its way safely around such a noisy, terrifying city?

"Wait till we get inside the stables," James said quietly to her. "We may get a chance to ask if anyone spotted a puppy yesterday."

It was a disappointing morning, though, as far as lost Labradors were concerned. Mandy and James both loved seeing the beautiful carriage horses, but none of the attendants had any news of a puppy having been reported around the Palace the day before. The stables were at the side of Buckingham Palace and backed onto the Palace grounds, so they kept their eyes open as they walked around. If the pup was still there, though, he didn't seem to want to be found.

After a couple of hours at the Royal Mews, they crossed the wide streets in front of the Palace and entered St. James's Park to meet the others for lunch. Mandy began to feel more cheerful as she looked at the view. There was a lake in the middle of the park, sparkling in the sun, with a pretty bridge across it. Ducks and a couple of majestic swans were swimming to and fro underneath.

"It's like being back in the country!" she said to James.

"According to my guidebook there used to be a herd of cows kept here," James replied. "They'd milk them on the spot if anyone was thirsty and charge a penny a glass. That was about three hundred years ago, though."

Dr. Emily laughed. "What would we do without you and your guidebook, James!" she said, putting an arm around his shoulders and making him blush.

As they headed across the grass toward the bandstand where they'd arranged to meet the others, Mandy heard a familiar voice booming out.

"I told the hotel manager that Pandora was extremely well behaved," Mrs. Ponsonby was saying. "After all, I trained her myself! There is no reason why she shouldn't be allowed into the dining room. If anyone wants to complain, I'll soon straighten them out!"

Mrs. Ponsonby was sitting in a deck chair next to Mandy's grandma, in the shade of some trees near the bandstand. Miss Davy and Mrs. McFarlane were with them, too, helping to lay out Mac's picnic on a blanket. Pandora was sitting on Mrs. Ponsonby's lap, staring at the food and drooling.

"Hello, everyone," Mandy said, dropping to her knees on the blanket and suddenly realizing she was starving. "This picnic looks great!"

"Oh, hello, dear!" her grandma said, taking some cartons of juice out of the bag. She looked very relieved to see them. "Have you had a good morning? I've been wondering when you were all going to get here."

"Hello there, Mandy and James! And the rest of the family, too, I see," Mrs. Ponsonby said, waving and smiling in a gracious manner. "So nice to see familiar faces in the middle of London. Of course, when I meet the Queen, her face will look very familiar! But that's not quite the same, is it?" She laughed loudly.

Mandy passed around the paper plates and helped herself to an egg roll. She sat back on the blanket, enjoying the fresh air and the warmth of the sun on her skin, listening to the others chatting quietly together. Gradually, though, she became aware of a strange snuffling sound above the background murmur. Pandora had jumped down from Mrs. Ponsonby's lap and was advancing steadily toward some sausages, her little pink tongue hanging out of her mouth.

"Uh-oh, Pandora's decided it's time for her lunch, too," Mandy said, moving the plate to a corner of the blanket out of the Peke's reach. She gave her a quick pat to make sure there were no hard feelings. Pandora shuffled back to her mistress's deck chair, looking put out.

"Never mind, my precious," Mrs. Ponsonby cooed, scooping her up again. "You'll have some lovely chicken from Mommy's plate in a minute."

Mandy and James exchanged glances. "No wonder Pandora wants to eat our picnic," Mandy whispered to James. "You'd think Mrs. Ponsonby would know better than to feed her like that."

"So what have the rest of you been up to while we've been inspecting the Queen's horses?" her father said, munching on a cheese and tomato sandwich.

"We spent a most enjoyable morning at the Maritime Museum," Miss Davy said. "It was very interesting, and the employees were charming. Mr. Pickard and Mr. Bell came, too."

Suddenly, Mandy froze, her roll halfway to her mouth. "James!" she hissed. "James! Look over there! And keep quiet!"

James had been about to pop open a bag of chips. He put it down and stared around, trying to figure out where Mandy was looking. And then his eyes widened as he caught sight of what she'd seen. From behind the large plane tree they were sitting under, an inquisitive little head was peeping out. A chocolate-brown head, with soft floppy ears and shining dark eyes.

"There he is!" Mandy whispered excitedly, sitting up on her heels. "That's our puppy!"

Six

As soon as he realized he'd been spotted, the little dog hid behind the tree again. Mandy held her breath, then released it slowly as she saw the Labrador's appealing face come back into view. Just like Pandora, he was staring hungrily at the sausages. Without realizing it, Mandy had brought the plate much closer to him when she'd moved it away from the Pekingese.

"We've got to take this slowly," she whispered to James. "He seems much more jumpy now than when we saw him at the Palace."

As casually as possible, she moved the plate of sausages almost within the puppy's reach, in order to tempt him out. Trying not to startle him, she watched out of the corner of her eye as the little dog put his head to one side and licked his lips hungrily. He looked quite thin now, and there were muddy patches on his bedraggled brown coat. The puppy must have been having a tough time, and Mandy felt her heart melt. They had to make sure he was safe and properly cared for.

But she had forgotten Pandora. The Peke had obviously decided those sausages belonged to her, and she was watching them jealously. Growling softly in her throat, she waddled forward over the blanket in hot pursuit of her escaping dinner. Unfortunately, the pup had chosen this very moment to pluck up his courage to dash out from the safety of the tree. He and Pandora came face-to-face. The young Labrador was already taller than the fat little Pekingese, but there was no doubt who was top dog. Pandora bristled, her silky cream coat quivering with fury like an indignant powder puff, and let out a stream of shrill yaps.

"Pandora! My precious!" Mrs. Ponsonby shrieked in alarm, struggling up from her deck chair to find out what was the matter.

It was all too much for the poor Labrador puppy. He turned tail and fled across the grass toward the bandstand.

Mandy was already on her feet. "Come on, James!"

she called, tearing off after the puppy. "We can't let him get away!"

Now that the pup was almost within their grasp, she was determined not to lose him again. She didn't want to alarm him even more by the chase, but they had to stop him once and for all. It was too dangerous for him to go running around on his own.

And then her eyes widened in horror. "James!" she called, gasping for breath. "Look where he's heading!"

The puppy was making straight for the huge ornamental gates at the side of the park, which were wide open. Beyond them, traffic was speeding along the busy street, and if they weren't careful, they could drive the puppy right into the path of the oncoming cars.

James waved, and Mandy knew he'd seen the danger. He veered around in a circle to the left so that the puppy wouldn't be frightened by someone running right behind him. Then he swung back to try to head the puppy off before he could reach the gate. It was hopeless, though. The dog was too fast, and they were both running out of steam — they just couldn't reach him in time.

Mandy could hardly bear to look as the pup headed for the inviting open gates in front of him. A couple of people were strolling casually past, and Mandy yelled,

"Stop the puppy! Please, somebody, stop him!" But no one seemed to hear.

And then, just as the little Labrador was about to dash through the gates, a large group of tourists appeared. They stood in a long line along the sidewalk with their backs to the park, chatting excitedly and taking photographs of Buckingham Palace.

Oh, thank goodness! Mandy said to herself. The gateway was blocked.

The Labrador skidded as he turned around in confusion, all long legs and oversized paws, and stood there, panting.

Mandy put on a final burst of speed. "Got you!" She gasped, flinging her arms around the puppy and holding his heaving, wriggling body tight to her chest.

"Well, he's not in too bad shape, considering he's been on the run for a few days," Dr. Adam said, straightening up after examining the pup and giving him a pat on the head.

"Are you sure he's okay?" Mandy asked. She could detect a note of hesitation in her father's voice. "Is anything wrong?"

"Well, I'm just a bit worried about his right ear," Dr. Adam replied. "Do you see how he keeps shaking his head? And there's a lot of wax there. I think he might have some kind of irritation inside."

"A grass seed, perhaps?" Dr. Emily said, looking over his shoulder. "Difficult to tell without an auriscope, isn't it?"

"Is that serious?" Mandy asked, looking intently at the puppy.

"It could be," her father replied. "Grass seeds work their way down the dog's ear canal, you see, because of their pointed shape. If they end up next to the eardrum they can cause a lot of pain or discomfort. We really need to get him to a vet right away so his ear can be examined with an auriscope, like your mother says."

"Poor little thing," Mandy said, petting the pup gently. He was still wary but seemed much less frightened now, and he lifted his head at the sound of her voice to lick her chin. "What will happen to him if there *is* something stuck in his ear?" she asked.

"He'll have to have a general anesthetic if there is an obstruction," Dr. Emily replied. "Just to keep him still while it's taken out."

"But how do we know where the nearest vet is?" James asked anxiously. "And what will happen to him after that?"

"Well, we could call the SPCA," Adam Hope sug-

gested. "They'll probably treat him and then take him to a center for stray dogs. They'll be able to find out there if he's been microchipped."

"Oh, I hope he has," Mandy said. She knew how much easier it was to reunite dogs with their owners if they'd had a specially coded microchip put into the scruff of their neck.

"Poor thing," Mandy's grandma said kindly, looking at the timid little dog. "It must all seem very strange to him."

"Couldn't we just take him to the shelter ourselves?" Mandy asked her father. "I'm sure they'll have a vet who could look at his ear. He's already becoming used to us, and it would be much less unsettling for him."

"Do you know, I've always wanted to visit a shelter!" Eileen Davy said enthusiastically. "Ever since I saw a television program about one. May I come along with you?"

"All right, all right!" Dr. Adam said, raising his hands in surrender. "I can see when I'm outnumbered. Why don't the four of us take the pup in? I'm sure a taxi driver would know where the shelter is. Then your mother can have time to shop this afternoon with Grandma."

"I've got your number, Adam Hope!" Dr. Emily laughed. "You'd do anything to get out of a shopping trip."

*　　　*　　　*

"Casey's going to be so annoyed that she missed out on this," Mandy said as she sat with James and Miss Davy in the back of a black London taxi on their way to the shelter. The puppy dozed on the seat between them, his head resting on his paws. Occasionally he whimpered and scratched his ear with his paw.

"We'll have to tell her all about it," James said, petting the puppy comfortingly. "By the way, what do you think about Brownie as a name for the puppy?" he went on. "Only for the moment, of course. He just reminds me so much of Blackie when he was little."

"Hmm, maybe." Mandy looked at the Labrador pup and tried to think of a way not to hurt James's feelings. "Blackie is the perfect name for Blackie, of course. But I'm not so sure about Brownie."

"Well, what about Bruno?" Miss Davy suggested. "Would you say that had more of a ring to it?"

"Perfect!" James and Mandy decided together.

"Now, don't go getting too attached to this puppy," Dr. Adam said, smiling at them from the pull-down seat opposite. "We're taking him to the shelter and leaving him there so that his owner can claim him. And we're not bringing any other strays back with us to Welford, Mandy, no matter how appealing they are."

"Don't worry, Dad." Mandy sighed. "I know the rule." There were too many animal patients at the Ark for the

Hopes to adopt any more as pets. Mandy understood that, even though it was hard to accept sometimes.

The taxi soon drew up outside the shelter. Dr. Adam paid the driver while James carried Bruno inside, holding him tightly, and Mandy followed with Miss Davy. The puppy looked around nervously, trembling a little at the roar of the traffic.

"He's so much jumpier now than he was when we first saw him," Mandy commented to Miss Davy. She'd already told her all about their first sighting of the pup at Buckingham Palace. "It makes you wonder what's been happening to him over the past couple of days."

"The poor creature must be terrified," Miss Davy said sympathetically, holding an inner door open so James could carry Bruno into the reception area.

Ten minutes later, they were all sitting in a side room with Penny, who took charge of the dogs that people brought in. The door was firmly shut, and Penny was giving the chocolate-brown Labrador time to sniff around and get the feel of the place while she asked Mandy and James how they'd found him. They told her all about it, and Dr. Adam told her about the puppy's ear problem, too.

"I'll get Frank to have a look at him right away," Penny said, completing the registration form.

After she had spoken to the center's vet on the phone,

she gazed thoughtfully at the puppy with her calm gray eyes. "It certainly looks like he's come from a good home," she commented. "But I checked the register earlier this morning, and I don't remember anyone having reported a missing Labrador. I'm surprised his owner hasn't called us or the police by now. Let me just check if he's been microchipped." She ran a scanner over the scruff of Bruno's neck. "No, nothing, I'm afraid," she said, shaking her head.

"What if his owner never gets in touch?" James asked. "What will happen to him then?"

"We'll keep him for seven days in the holding kennel," Penny replied, taking a collar with a numbered identification disk and buckling it around Bruno's neck. "If his owner hasn't turned up to claim him by then, he'll be moved over to the sale block so we can find him a new home."

"Oh, Bruno!" Mandy said, unable to resist giving him another cuddle. "How could anybody bear to part with you?"

"Don't worry," Penny smiled. "We'll take good care of him. If he isn't claimed, we'll make sure he goes to a new family who'll look after him well. He won't be with us for long, I'm sure." She snapped a leash onto the puppy's collar and stood up. "Now then, Bruno, are you going to show me how well you walk to heel? Let's go and find your cage! Then our vet can come and have a look at you. He's on his rounds now."

"May we come, too?" Mandy asked. "Just to make sure he's okay?" She'd formed a real bond with this little puppy from the moment she'd first set eyes on him, and she was sure James felt the same. Saying good-bye was going to be very hard.

"Of course," Penny said, looking at their sad faces. "Why don't you all come, and then afterward I can show you some of the other dogs? We've got cats, too, though you might not have realized. They're much quieter!"

"That sounds like a good idea," Dr. Adam replied, putting a comforting arm around Mandy's shoulders. "Let's go to see Bruno's new apartment!"

As they approached the kennel area, Mandy could hear the sound of barking. It rose to a crescendo when Penny opened the door and showed them into a room lined on both sides with cages. They held about fifty dogs of all shapes and sizes. Some crowded up against the wire, yapping like crazy, while others stayed in their baskets, looking out silently with nervous eyes. Bruno shrank back from the noise, so Penny scooped him up and carried him as she walked toward an empty cage.

"These are the dogs that have been brought in today," she said to James and Mandy over the din, pointing to the cages along one side of the room. "The summer is our busiest time, I'm afraid. Some people don't bother to make the right arrangements for their pets when they go on vacation. They just turn them out on the street to fend for themselves."

"They shouldn't be allowed to keep animals ever again," Mandy said fiercely. Cruelty like that was something she would never understand or forgive. It made her blood boil.

Bruno was beginning to struggle in Penny's arms, so she handed him to Mandy and said, "Would you like to put him in his basket? I think he's more used to you than he is to me." She opened the door of the cage and stood back to let Mandy and James take Bruno inside. "Don't worry, the vet will be here any minute," she added reassuringly.

"We'll wait here," Dr. Adam said as he and Miss Davy looked on. "We don't want to crowd him."

Mandy carefully settled the puppy into his basket. James knelt down beside her, giving Bruno a farewell pat before taking one last photograph for his collection.

"There you are, Bruno," Mandy said encouragingly, arranging his blanket comfortably and trying to swallow the lump in her throat. She kissed the top of his satin-smooth head and whispered, "It was nice knowing you. Good-bye, and good luck!"

Seven

"Now, come on, you two," Dr. Adam said to James and Mandy, clapping an arm around their shoulders. "There's no need to be upset. I bet Bruno's owner will come to get him soon. He's in exactly the right place, and you've done the best for him you possibly could. So cheer up!"

"That's right," Miss Davy added. "And remember what Penny's told you — even if his owner doesn't turn up, plenty of people will want to give Bruno a good home."

"I suppose so," Mandy said, blinking away her tears. "It's just strange leaving him here without knowing what's going to happen."

"Well, you can always call me in a few days to see if there's any news," Penny said, leading them out of the room. "I'm sure we'll be able to rehome Bruno very quickly if we have to. Everyone wants a puppy, especially a purebred. It's a pity, really. So many of our older mongrels make wonderful family pets. Training an excitable puppy takes lots more time and patience."

"That's true," James said, and Mandy could tell exactly whom he was thinking of. "I've got a black Labrador at home, and he doesn't always do as he's told, even now that he's full grown!"

Penny took them over to what she called the "sale block." "These are the dogs that are waiting to be rehomed," she told them over a chorus of barks. "We'll keep them for as long as it takes."

"How could anyone choose between them?" Mandy wondered as she passed cage after cage. German shepherds, terriers, greyhounds, and more varieties of mixed-breed dogs than she could ever have imagined rushed up to greet the visitors. Most of them were barking and wagging their tails furiously, as if pleading for a chance to show just what wonderful pets they would make.

"I'd like to take them all home — every one," James said as an eager mongrel tried to lick his fingers through the wire of the cage. "I don't know what Blackie would think about it, though!"

"I sometimes think it's the dogs that pick their owners," Penny said. "You'll often find that a dog will react to one particular person very strongly." She smiled at the mongrel James was petting. "This little fellow loves everyone, though," she added.

"Do you ever get depressed, working here?" Mandy asked. She was finding the sight of so many abandoned dogs, desperate for a home, absolutely heartbreaking.

"Not often," Penny replied. "This is a very happy place, most of the time! Seeing an animal go to a new home where you know he'll be loved makes all the difficult times worthwhile. But I do get angry at the state some of the poor things are in when they come to us. And it's sad to see some of our old-timers still here, month after month. Like Spike, for instance."

She pointed to a large gray dog, curled up in his basket. He opened one eye as they came up to the cage and lifted his head to watch them, but he made no attempt to get up. "Spike is the sweetest, gentlest creature you could imagine," Penny explained. "But as soon as people find out how old he is, they don't want to know."

"I can't stand that kind of attitude," Miss Davy said, and Mandy was surprised by the depth of feeling in her voice. "It's the same with people. Once you've passed a certain age, it's as though you're not good for anything anymore. But look at that lovely dog — he's got so much to offer."

Spike raised his ears and looked at her. Then, slowly, he began to struggle stiffly to his feet.

"Now, that's a surprise," Penny said quietly. "He doesn't usually bother to get up. It's as though he's given up hope of anyone taking an interest in him."

Spike climbed out of the basket and padded toward them.

"Does he have some greyhound in him?" James asked. "Look at those long legs! I bet he can run fast."

Penny was too busy watching Spike to answer. He'd walked up to the cage door and was sitting there, staring intently at Eileen Davy and slowly wagging the very tip of his tail. Then he barked — just once — and turned to look at Penny. "Well, how about that?" she said in astonishment.

"Could he come out of the cage for a second?" Mandy asked. "It would be nice for Spike to have a fuss made over him for once." An idea was taking shape in her head. Hadn't Penny said the dogs sometimes chose their owners? From what she could see, it certainly looked as though Spike had chosen Miss Davy. Perhaps it would only take a little encouragement for her to fall for him, too.

"Okay," Penny said, already opening the cage door. "I'm sure he'd love a bit of attention."

Spike made a beeline for Miss Davy as soon as he was out of the cage. He pushed his head against her smart navy skirt, shedding a couple of pale hairs. Then he sat in front of her and solemnly offered a paw to shake.

"Oh, he's gorgeous, isn't he?" Mandy said. "He's really taken to you, Miss Davy."

"He definitely has," Penny said. "I've never seen him behave like this before!"

Eileen Davy held Spike's paw and gazed into his appealing eyes. "I can guess exactly what's going through your mind, Mandy," she said in a voice that was rather softer than usual. "But it's no use, I'm afraid. You can't just adopt a dog on a whim. It's a big commitment, and not one I'm ready to make just now."

"Oh, Spike would be so happy —" Mandy began, but her father quietly interrupted her by laying his hands firmly on her shoulders.

"Mandy, Miss Davy is right," he told her firmly. "You can't force someone into a decision like this. Not to mention all the practical difficulties! We're on vacation, remember, and we only came here to hand Bruno over. Now I think it's time for us to go."

Mandy could hardly bear to watch as Penny led Spike back into his cage. She could feel his eyes burning into her back as they turned away and hear his deep, urgent bark follow them out of the kennel block. *Don't leave me here!* he seemed to be calling. *Just give me a chance!*

They were all quiet on the journey back to the Crow's Nest. Miss Davy stared out of the train window, lost in thought. Dr. Adam fell asleep, and James read his guidebook. Mandy closed her eyes and let images from the shelter whirl around inside her head. She tried to think positively. Bruno would be well looked after there, she knew that, and if his owner didn't claim him, Penny would make sure he went to a good home. By the time the train had pulled into Greenwich station, she had convinced herself that Spike would also find a loving family soon. It was too painful to imagine him left at the center for much longer.

They found Casey sitting in the backyard of the Crow's Nest. "You'll never guess what's happened!" Mandy told her. "We've got the most amazing news!"

Casey laid down the book she'd been reading and squinted up at them from under her baseball cap. "We've all been invited to tea at Buckingham Palace?" she said. "Big Ben has stopped telling time? They've caught a shark in the Thames?"

"We found the puppy!" James announced triumphantly, sitting next to her on the bench. "We were having a picnic in the park, and there he was!"

"That's great!" Casey exclaimed. "But it's not so great that I wasn't there! Why didn't you come back and get me?"

"There just wasn't time for that." Mandy smiled. "We managed to catch him, and then we took him straight to a shelter. They're going to see if anyone claims him, and if not they'll find him a new home. We've given him a name, too — Bruno."

"Oh, I wish I could take him back to the States!" Casey sighed. "I feel like Bruno belongs to us, don't you? What was he like? Was he just as cute close-up?"

"He was adorable," Mandy said. "Wasn't he, James? It was so hard to part with him." She fell silent, remembering how she'd felt as they walked away from the shelter. There had been two dogs she hated to leave behind, not just one.

"So what's been happening here?" James asked Casey. "What have you done today?"

"Not much," she replied with a huge yawn. "Certainly nothing as exciting as that. We hung around here in the morning, and then we went shopping in the market this afternoon."

"That's what Mom and Grandma went to do, with Mrs. McFarlane," Mandy said, looking at her watch. "Aren't they back?"

"Nope, nobody's here except for us and Mac," Casey replied. "He's in the kitchen, I think. But listen, I haven't told you the good news. Dad says I'm okay, so I can come to the Millennium Dome with you tomorrow."

"That's great!" James said. "I can't wait to see it."

Then a thoughtful look came over his face. "Do you realize, Mandy," he continued, "we've only got two full days left in London? The time's going so quickly!"

"I know," Mandy said. "But then on the other hand, I feel as if we've been here forever." She looked around the sunny garden. Patch, the little tortoiseshell cat, was stalking through some tall grass in the border like a miniature tiger. And there, in the shade of an overhanging lilac tree, stood Sinbad's cage.

"Oh, Sinbad's here!" she said, going up to say hello. "He's lost his voice all of a sudden."

"You'll be shocked when you see him," Casey warned, getting up to follow Mandy.

Sinbad was sitting on the perch with his back toward them, but he turned around and whistled as they approached. "Oh, no!" Mandy gasped, horrified. "Sinbad, what's happened to you?"

There were hardly any gray feathers left on his breast, and he'd even plucked away some of the down beneath so that bare skin showed through. He was a pathetic sight — a bedraggled, scrappy-looking creature. "Hello, Sinbad," he squawked, as if he were trying to pretend nothing was wrong. Then he turned away again, as though too embarrassed to meet Mandy's eye.

"Mac found him like that in the dining room this afternoon," Casey said. "He's really worried."

James had come over to join them. "Why on earth would Sinbad want to do that to himself?" he asked. "It looks really sore!"

Mandy tried to remember what her mother had said. "Apparently it's because he's under some kind of stress," she said, thinking hard. "But we have no idea what's causing it."

"You don't think Patch could be frightening him?" James asked. "Cats do hunt birds, don't they? Perhaps he thinks she's after him."

Casey shook her head. "No, Mac told me they get along really well," she said. "Sinbad was here first, and he soon showed Patch who was boss. They're the best of friends now."

Mandy remembered the first time they'd met Sinbad. It seemed ridiculous now to think that they'd been so frightened. Surely it couldn't just have been one parrot all by itself that had made them feel like that. What else was there? "Come on!" she said suddenly. "I think we need to go to the dining room."

"Why?" Casey asked as Mandy hurried them inside. "What's in there that we have to see in such a rush?"

"I'm not sure yet," Mandy replied, throwing open the door. "But I think we need to get inside Sinbad's skin. There's something in this room that's making him uncomfortable, I'm sure of it. We felt it, too, James, the first time we met him. We were scared, and it wasn't just because he was squawking at us."

The three of them stared around the room. Then they all looked back at one another and said at exactly the same time, "Daisy May!"

"She's wonderful, isn't she?" Mac said, passing by on his way out of the kitchen with a tray of tea. "I got her in the antiques market a couple of months ago."

"No, you don't understand!" Mandy said, stumbling in her eagerness to get the words out. "That's why Sinbad is so unhappy. He's on his own with her for most of the day, and he doesn't like it."

Mac stared at her for a few seconds without speaking. "Do you think so?" he said eventually. "Come on, she's only a carving. I think she's beautiful."

"She *is* beautiful," Mandy replied eagerly, pulling him into the dining room to face the figurehead. "But, look — don't you think she's a bit threatening, too? Sinbad doesn't know she's not real. I think he's terrified of her."

"We're certain that's it!" Casey added, speaking for all three of them.

"I suppose he does spend most of his time in here," Mac said, putting the tray down on a side table and scratching his beard while he looked at Daisy May. He sighed. "It was a big job getting her up on that wall. But if it'll help Sinbad, she'll just have to come down again."

"But Sinbad's cage is on wheels," James said. "Why don't you put him somewhere else for the time being and see what happens?"

"Like the hall," Mandy suggested, remembering the first time they'd seen Patch hiding behind the globe. "There's so much to look at there, and people are coming and going all day. He'd get lots of attention!"

"Of course!" Mac said. "I've just gotten so used to Sinbad being in this room that I've never considered moving him. But maybe he is a bit lonely in here. And come to think of it, he did take a turn for the worse around the time that Daisy May arrived. I wonder if you could be right."

"Oh, I hope we are," Mandy said, thinking of the poor moth-eaten parrot out in the garden. "We can't let Sinbad keep on hurting himself!"

Eight

Mandy woke up the next morning to sunlight streaming in through her curtains and a strange sound floating up from downstairs. She quickly pulled some clothes on, trying not to disturb her grandmother, who was still asleep, and crept out of the room.

"The sun has got his hat on," Sinbad was squawking merrily, "hip, hip, hip, hooray! The sun has got his hat on, and he's coming out today." Mac had moved away a coatrack and put the parrot's cage in a corner of the hall, near a side window that looked out on the street.

"Hello there, Sinbad," she said, smiling at him through the bars. "You're feeling very chirpy today, aren't you?"

"Hello, Sinbad!" the parrot replied, walking carefully down the perch to greet her. "What a fine fellow!"

"Well, maybe not quite yet, but I'm sure you soon will be," Mandy promised. "I think you like it better here, don't you?"

"Oh, he's a different bird already," Mac said, coming into the hall with a tea towel over his shoulder. "This is the perfect place for him! It's not too drafty, and he can watch what's going on outside, too. He's already made friends with the mailman."

"Mac! Mac!" Sinbad ordered as soon as he caught sight of his owner. "Come here, boy."

"That means he wants a tickle," Mac told Mandy. "I'm busy," he called back to the parrot, but Sinbad just squawked his name again — even louder this time.

"Okay, you old rascal," Mac replied, putting down the towel and going over to open the cage door. Gently, he reached in to scratch the tiny feathers that overlapped each other like silvery chain mail on the top of Sinbad's head. "I'm just kicking myself for not having thought of it before," he went on. "Sinbad's back to his old self, even if he is going to look a mess for a while longer. Thanks for solving the mystery, Mandy."

"Oh, I'm just glad he seems to be better," she said. "Let's hope those feathers don't take too long to grow back."

"You can get a cardboard collar from the vet's," Dr. Emily advised Mac, overhearing their conversation as she came down the stairs. "Just to make sure he gets out of the habit of pecking himself."

"I will," Mac said, walking back toward the kitchen. "Just as soon as I've finished the breakfasts. I thought we'd have waffles this morning, to celebrate."

"We're going to miss Mac's cooking," Grandma said, putting an arm around Mandy's shoulders. "But just look at this parrot! He certainly seems to like it here in the hall."

Sinbad walked back down the perch and then suddenly picked his way up a rope at the side of the cage to swing upside down from the top, hooking his claws through the bars. "Hello, Sinbad," he squawked again, looking cheekily back and making them both laugh.

"So, Mandy, there's nothing left for you to worry about," her mother said, giving her a squeeze. "Sinbad's going to get better, and you found your runaway pup. Now you can really enjoy the last couple of days here."

"I will!" Mandy replied, turning away from the cage. "I wish we could have seen Bruno back together with his owner, but at least we know he's safe."

"And we're going to visit the Dome today," her mother reminded her. "I can't wait to see what it's like inside!"

*   *   *

A couple of hours later, full of waffles and maple syrup, everyone wandered down the street to catch a bus that would take them the short distance to the Dome.

"Are Walter and Ernie coming?" Mandy asked her grandmother as they waited at the bus stop. "We've hardly seen them this vacation."

"Yes, we're going to meet them outside the Dome at ten, along with Mrs. McFarlane," her grandma replied. "I called the pub last night to arrange it." She laughed. "I think they've had enough of city life. Ernie said he would never have guessed how noisy London was."

"You know, I'm looking forward to going back, too," Casey confided to Mandy and James. "We've had a great time here, and I'm so glad I've met you both, but there's no place like home, is there?"

"No, there isn't," Mandy agreed, thinking wistfully about Animal Ark. She looked around the bustling street, thronging with traffic and overlooked by town-houses and apartment buildings. How different her life would have been if she'd been adopted by a family who lived in the city! It made her dizzy just thinking about it.

Then a huddled figure sitting in a doorway near the bus stop caught her eye. "Buy a magazine and help the home-less?" the man asked, waving a copy in her direction.

"Sure," Mandy said, fumbling for her purse. She still

had most of her spending money left, and besides, they'd just been talking about how much they were all looking forward to going home. Here was someone who didn't have a home at all, and Mandy wanted to help.

"Thanks, dear," said the man, handing over the magazine. "Have a nice day! Where are you going?"

"We're going to the Millennium Dome," Mandy said. "Oh, can I say hello to your dog?" A bright-looking little terrier was sleeping on a blanket at the man's feet.

"Course you can," he replied, tucking Mandy's coin away in his pocket. "She won't bite. Her name's Lucy, if you want to introduce yourself. And I'm Joe."

"Hello, Lucy," Mandy said solemnly, patting the dog's head. "My name's Mandy. It's nice to meet you."

James and Casey came over to join them, and they each bought a magazine, too. Lucy wagged her stumpy tail a mile a minute, delighted with all the attention she was getting.

"Oh, she's gorgeous!" Casey said to Joe. "If she's not careful, she'll wag that tail right off!"

"How long have you had her?" Mandy asked.

"I found her in a garbage can last year," Joe said, petting his dog with a grimy hand. "Someone had dumped her, along with the rubbish. But I took her to the animal hospital, and she's fine now. We're company for each other, Lucy and me. I wouldn't be without her for anything."

"It must be hard to look after her sometimes," James said shyly. "I mean, if she's ill or anything."

"We get by," Joe said. "She's had all her shots, and I take her back to the animal hospital if she has any problems. It's easier in the summer, but we make it through the winter as best we can. She's a good little hot-water bottle, that's for sure!" He looked over at the bus stop. "Oh, it looks like that's your bus. Better not miss it!"

Mandy's parents were calling them. "Coming!" Mandy shouted back. She looked at the money in her purse. Suddenly, the idea of spending it on tacky plastic souvenirs didn't seem such a good one. "Here," she said, giving Joe some paper money. "Can you put this toward a coat for Lucy? She might be glad to have one when it gets colder."

"Well, thanks very much," said Joe, delighted. His smile grew even broader when James and Casey added their own money to the collection. "She'll have the warmest coat in London this winter," he promised, holding Lucy up and waving good-bye as they got on the bus. "Come and visit again and you'll see!"

They waved back out of the window as the bus pulled away. "It's great to come across someone who really cares about his dog," James commented as Joe and Lucy grew smaller in the distance. "Especially after all those poor strays we saw yesterday."

"I was just thinking exactly the same thing," Mandy agreed. "Lucy might not have regular meals or a warm bed, but I'd say she was a lot better off than Spike. She has someone who loves her, and that's more important than anything."

"Look, there's the Dome!" Mandy's dad said as the

white mushroom shape, familiar from so many photographs, came into view. But Mandy was still thinking about Spike. She hoped he and Bruno would soon have owners to love them as much as Joe obviously loved Lucy. But somehow she wasn't convinced.

Nine

"Now, what are we going to do on our last day in London?" Dr. Adam asked, looking around the breakfast table the following morning.

"It's a pity the weather's not better," said Mandy's grandmother, gazing out at the cloudy sky. "Mrs. Ponsonby's got her famous garden party this afternoon. I hope her new hat doesn't get wet, or we'll never hear the end of it!"

"Why don't we take a bus trip around London?" James suggested. "I noticed special sight-seeing buses at the station. You can get on and off them wherever you like, and they take you to all the famous places." Suddenly, realizing that everyone's eyes were on him, he stopped and looked rather embarrassed. "But I don't mind if no one else wants to," he said. "It's just an idea."

"Well, I think it's a very good one," Dr. Emily said, draining her cup of tea. "We had such a busy time yesterday. Watching the world go by from a seat on the bus is just what I feel like doing!"

"Me, too," Mandy said. "Why don't we all go? I'm sure the Baxters would like to come, and we *have* to spend our last day with Casey. We could get Walter and Ernie to come along, too, and Miss Davy and Mrs. McFarlane. Then we could all go out for a meal this evening. What do you say, Grandma?"

"I'd say you two had better plan next year's trip!" laughed her grandmother. "It all sounds perfect, dear. I'll give Walter and Ernie a call — I'm sure they'd love to come."

It didn't seem long before everyone was sitting upstairs on the open top deck of a sight-seeing bus. The sun was just breaking through the clouds as they pulled away to start the tour.

"Would you just look at that traffic!" Ernie said, looking down at the street as they approached Trafalgar Square. "Those cars are packed solid!"

"Where are we now?" Casey asked James. "I didn't

hear what the guide said. What's that big pillar coming up?"

"That's Nelson's Column," James replied. "This is one of the places I thought we could stop at for a while. I really want to take some photos of those big stone lions at the bottom."

"Sounds good to me," Mandy said, getting up from her seat as the bus stopped. "Who's coming?"

It turned out that everyone wanted to see the lions at the foot of Nelson's Column and wander around Trafalgar Square. There were flocks of pigeons everywhere and even a couple of seagulls, wheeling around the fountains. After James had taken a few shots, he decided to get everyone together for a group picture. "Mr. Pickard and Mr. Bell, could you stand at the back?" he called. "Then Mandy and Casey in the middle, please, with everyone else sort of gathered around."

"Do you want my cap on or off?" Walter Pickard called out obligingly.

"Off, I think," James replied from behind the camera. But then, instead of taking the photo, he lowered his camera and stood peering at something behind them.

"Oh, come on, James!" Mandy called impatiently. "We've been standing here forever. Hurry up and take the picture so I can go and feed the pigeons!"

But James continued to stand still, holding the camera loosely by his side and staring at the fountain be-hind them on the other side of the square. "I don't be-lieve it!" he said, pointing.

Mandy turned to look. She rubbed her eyes and looked again. It couldn't be true! But there, splashing happily around in the fountain, was a mischievous little brown Labrador puppy. "Bruno!" she gasped in amaze-ment. "But that's impossible!"

"Now this is someone I have to meet!" Casey said, striding toward the fountain. "After all, I missed out last time."

"Careful, Casey!" Mandy warned, rushing along after her. "He's quite nervous, and he could easily run out into the street. There are cars everywhere!"

The puppy was romping through the shallow water, sending up showers of spray and drenching a small group of tourists who had gathered to watch him play. They didn't seem to mind, though. Cameras were click-ing, and everyone was smiling at the adorable little dog.

"Here, boy!" Casey whistled. "Come here, Bruno."

To Mandy's surprise, the puppy splashed obediently toward her, pink tongue hanging out of one side of his mouth as he bounded over.

"Well, you're not nervous with me, are you?" Casey said as she petted him. "You are *so* cute! I don't even mind that you're soaking me."

Mandy stared at the Labrador pup, still hardly able to take in what she was seeing. There were a few muddy patches on his damp coat, but he seemed to be in good spirits and otherwise unhurt.

"You should keep your dog on a leash," an elderly woman said severely to Mandy, turning back to look disapprovingly at Casey over the top of her glasses. "He could cause a bad accident."

"He's not exactly our dog," Mandy began, unable to

take her eyes off the puppy. Casey was holding him securely while he shook himself, sending silver droplets of water flying through the air. By now, Mandy's parents and the Baxters had come over, followed by Miss Davy and the others.

"Pass me your tie, please, Dad," Casey asked her father. "We need an emergency leash here."

"What on earth is this little fellow doing here?" Dr. Adam asked. "The last time we saw him, he was safely in his cage at the shelter!" He gave the puppy a quick examination. "Well, his ear seems fine now," he said. "That's something, I suppose."

"We'll have to tell the shelter we've found him again," Mandy said, crouching down to have a good look at Bruno as he sat by Casey's feet, the tip of his tail wagging furiously. "He must have escaped somehow."

"But how did he find his way here?" James wondered. "Think of all the traffic he had to get through."

"Well, however he managed it, I think we need to take him back to the shelter right away, don't you?" Miss Davy said. "They must be very worried about him being missing. Come on, this time it's my turn to pay for the taxi." And she started walking toward the road to look for one.

"What about our sight-seeing trip?" Ernie said. "There's another bus over there — we could catch it."

"Why don't the rest of you go on without us?" Dr. Adam replied. "Let's arrange to meet again at that café in St. James's Park for lunch. About one o'clock?"

"Well, if you're sure you don't mind taking care of our daughter," said Dr. Baxter. "And, Casey, that's my favorite tie. I want it back!"

Miss Davy soon managed to hail a taxi, and everyone went over toward it. The little pup bounded along at Casey's side, quite happy to come along with them. Miss Davy held open the door, and he hopped in and sat on the backseat as though he'd been riding in taxis all his life.

The taxi driver muttered something grumpily. "You'll have to squeeze in," he said over his shoulder in a louder voice. "Five passengers is the most I'm allowed to take, and that's not counting any dogs. And I hope he's not making a mess of my upholstery."

"Come on, Bruno," Mandy said, scooping him onto her lap. "You'd better sit here with me." She laid her cheek against his smooth brown head and added, "No more running off on your own now, okay?"

"There's something really strange about this," Mandy said as they waited for Penny to meet them in the reception area at the shelter. She took another long look at the puppy, which was busy winding Dr. Baxter's best tie into knots as he explored an interesting corner behind the chair.

"You're telling me!" James replied. "I still can't believe Bruno managed to get all the way from here to Trafalgar Square. It's on the other side of the river!"

"And without getting run over or caught," said Mandy's father. "That really is incredible. Maybe someone befriended him, but then why didn't they take him to a police station?"

"There's something else, though," Mandy went on. "He seems so different now — much more confident and bouncy. Look how easy it was to catch him. He got really spooked when we went after him on Monday." She clicked her fingers and the pup immediately came running up to sniff them. "See what I mean?" she said.

"It's because I'm here, of course," Casey joked, giving the pup a cuddle. "I've got a way with dogs. If I'd been around last time, you wouldn't have had any problems."

Before Mandy could think of a witty reply, Penny appeared. "Well, hello again," she said. "Have you come to visit Bruno? He's still feeling pretty miserable, I'm afraid."

"What do you mean?" James replied. He pointed toward the puppy, which had started to run in circles around Casey's feet. "Look! Bruno's here with us."

Penny jumped as soon as she caught sight of the little

dog. "But that's impossible!" she exclaimed. "I don't believe it!"

"Neither could we," Mandy said. "We just found him splashing around in the fountain in Trafalgar Square. Didn't you know he was missing?"

"He isn't missing, though!" Penny said. "I just walked past Bruno, asleep in his cage in the holding kennel. You were right, by the way — he did have a grass seed in his ear. We got it out just in time." She gave the puppy a pat, looking intently at him. "Well," she said, smiling at their astonished faces, "this little fellow's just as gorgeous, but he's not our Bruno."

They all stared at her for a moment, unable to take in this amazing piece of news.

"So that's why you thought there was something different about him, Mandy," said Dr. Adam. "He's a different dog!"

"Which means there are two lost puppies," Mandy said slowly. "And we've found both of them."

The pup began to wind his makeshift leash around Casey's legs, worrying away at it with sharp white teeth. "Hold on there, fella," she said. "My dad's going to kill me if you eat his tie."

"I think you'd better come with me, and we'll check him in," Penny said, bending down to give the puppy a quick examination. "Then we can give him a real collar and his own number. It'll be hard to tell him and Bruno apart."

"They must be from the same litter, don't you think?" Mandy said, crouching down beside her. "Same age, same coloring. And Trafalgar Square isn't that far from St. James's Park — where we picked up Bruno."

"So no one's reported losing any Labrador puppies yet?" Miss Davy asked.

"No, they haven't," Penny replied, giving the puppy a final pat and straightening up. "I really can't understand it. These two have obviously come from a good home, and they're so appealing. They should have been claimed immediately, but no one's contacted the police or the SPCA or any of the local vets. It's very strange."

It certainly is, Mandy thought. *If those two puppies belonged to me, I wouldn't let them out of my sight!*

"I'll just check this pup in, and then we can take him to see Bruno," Penny continued. "Come with me, and we'll get the forms filled out. I'm sure you remember the process from last time!"

"Perhaps we should call him Nelson for the time being," James suggested as they followed Penny into the main part of the home. "After all, we were standing by Nelson's Column when we saw him. Nelson and Bruno — what do you think?"

"I think that sounds great," Mandy replied, looking at

the bouncy little pup as he scampered along beside them, nose to the ground in search of interesting smells. "Nelson really suits him somehow."

"Nelson it is," Casey said, giving James a pat on the back.

"Who knows, maybe their owner will turn up soon, and we'll find out what their real names are," Penny added over her shoulder.

"Oh, I hope so." Mandy sighed. She couldn't shake off the feeling that someone, somewhere, must be desperate to find both Nelson and his brother.

"Well, those two are certainly happy to see each other!" Casey commented as they watched the two puppies playing together. As soon as Bruno had caught sight of Nelson, he'd rushed up to the cage door and thrown himself against it, whining and barking excitedly. Now the two of them were tearing around the kennel, wrestling each other to the ground, with lots of playful nips and growls. James took photo after photo until he ran out of Polaroid film.

"Bruno'll be so much happier to have some company," Mandy said. "Leaving him behind doesn't feel as bad now that Nelson's with him."

"I promise I'll call you and tell you what happens to

them," Penny said as she bolted the cage door. "When are you going home?"

"Tomorrow morning," Mandy said. "And Casey and her parents are leaving the day after that." She took one long last look at the two puppies, now curled up together on the blanket. "Oh, I hope they'll be okay!"

"We'll look after them, don't worry," Penny reassured her as they began to walk away.

"Actually, there is just one more thing," Miss Davy said, and something about the tone of her voice made everyone stop and look at her. "I don't want to hold you all up," she went on, taking a deep breath, "but I would like to see Spike again before we go."

"Oh, Miss Davy!" Mandy breathed, hardly daring to hope. "You don't mean —"

"Yes, I do," Eileen Davy said firmly. She turned to Penny. "I've been thinking this over very carefully, and I *would* like to offer him a home. If you think mine would be suitable, that is."

Before Penny could say anything in reply, Mandy had thrown her arms around Miss Davy and given her a big hug. "Oh, that's wonderful!" she cried. "He'll be so happy with you, I know he will! We'll help you walk him, and Mom and Dad can look after him in the clinic if he needs anything —"

"Calm down, Mandy!" Miss Davy said, though her eyes were shining and she didn't look at all cross. "I'm sure there are a lot of questions Penny needs to ask. I haven't been approved yet! But I haven't been able to get that dear old dog out of my mind, and coming back here for the second time seems like fate. I think I'm meant to have him."

Penny was smiling, too. "You're right, there are a lot of things we need to discuss," she said. "But I'm delighted you feel this way, and Spike will be, too. I'm sure we can work it all out!"

"That's marvelous news, Eileen," Dr. Adam said, and soon everyone was patting Miss Davy on the back and shaking her hand.

"Even if everything goes smoothly, you won't be able to take him right away, I'm afraid," Penny warned. "But we can certainly start the ball rolling now. Come back to my office for a moment, and we'll get going on the forms."

"Why don't we wait for you in the café here?" Mandy's dad suggested. "I could do with a cup of tea after all this excitement!"

They were just finishing their drinks by the time Miss Davy came back. She looked as neat and composed as usual, but underneath, Mandy could tell she was feeling very emotional. "Well, someone from the shelter is going to visit me next week," she informed them. "If all goes well, I could have Spike with me in Welford by the end of the month. There are my hens to consider, of course, but Penny tells me he's much too good to chase them. He really is the most delightful dog!"

"And we'd never have met him if it wasn't for the puppies," Mandy said, "Oh, Miss Davy, you are lucky!" She turned to her father, determined to try one question out on him, although she already had a very good idea what the answer would be.

"Dad," she began, "if the puppies' owner doesn't turn up, do you think there's any way —"

"No, Mandy, I'm sorry," her father replied firmly. "Hold it right there. They're beautiful dogs, but there's no way we can take them on. I know it seems hard, but we just can't —"

"Oh, thank goodness I caught you before you left!" Penny came bursting through the swinging doors and rushed up to their table. She sank down on a chair next to them to catch her breath. "I've just had a call from a woman who's lost her puppies," she went on. "They're Labradors — chocolate-colored ones. I think we've found Nelson and Bruno's owner! She's on her way over here now, and she wants to talk to you. Can you wait?"

Ten

"Oh, please, can we stay here a little longer?" Mandy begged her father. "I couldn't stand not knowing whether Nelson and Bruno really have been claimed!"

"Of course," Dr. Adam replied. "We've come this far. We might as well find out how the story ends." He looked at his watch and added, "We might be a bit late meeting the others for lunch, but I'm sure they won't mind waiting."

"Don't worry," said Miss Davy, getting to her feet. "I'll go to the park and let them know you've been delayed. To be honest, I want to share my good news with everyone. You can tell me later what happens with the puppies."

"Their owner — if she really is their owner — doesn't live far away," Penny said, after Miss Davy had left. "It won't take her very long to get here. Apparently she's a famous writer, though I hadn't heard of her. Jane, our switchboard operator, recognized the name." She looked down at the notepad she was holding. "Where is it, now? Yes, here we are. Laura Dawson."

"What?" James and Mandy exclaimed together. "Laura Dawson? Not *the* Laura Dawson?"

"Looks like it," Penny said, grinning at their startled faces. "Jane says her son's a big fan. He's got all the books she's ever written."

"You know Laura Dawson!" Mandy said excitedly, turning to Casey. "She's the author of all those fantastic animal stories — the Sweetwater Sanctuary series and the Running Wild books, and lots of others. You're reading one of hers now. I saw you, in the garden the other day."

"Of course!" Casey said. "So that's why her name sounded familiar. Wow! It's such a great story, and I'm gong to meet the person who wrote it! Now I really do have something to tell everyone back home."

Mandy stared into the distance. "To think that we

might actually have rescued Laura Dawson's puppies," she said in a faraway voice. "I can't believe it."

"Well, it sounds like she could do with some advice on looking after them," said Dr. Emily, "brilliant writer or not."

"I agree," Penny said. "There are a few things we need to ask Laura Dawson when she arrives. If Nelson and Bruno do belong to her, she's lucky to be getting them back in one piece."

"There has to be some explanation," Mandy said stubbornly. Laura Dawson was her favorite author. She wrote so beautifully about animals — surely she knew how to take care of her own?

Fifteen minutes later, a slim, anxious-looking woman with a large bag slung over one shoulder came rushing into the shelter. The swinging doors banged noisily behind her. James, Casey, Dr. Adam, and Mandy had moved from the café to wait for Laura Dawson in the reception area, and Mandy realized immediately that the famous writer had just arrived. She'd once seen her photograph on a poster in a bookshop.

"My name is Laura Dawson," the woman said, hurrying up to the reception desk. "I think you may have my puppies."

Mandy felt James nudge her side urgently. "There she is!" he hissed. "Go on, say something!"

"Take a seat, and someone will be with you shortly," the receptionist answered calmly, picking up her phone.

Laura Dawson walked toward them. Mandy had a quick impression of piercing blue eyes, fair skin, and dark wavy hair gathered back into a loose braid. "Um, Ms. Dawson," she began, standing up. "We, er, found your puppies and brought them here. If they are yours, that is. I'm Mandy Hope, and these are my friends James and Casey, and my father —"

"Oh, Mandy, I'm so glad to meet you!" Laura Dawson said. She smiled hello at all of them and then took Mandy's hand in her own for a moment. "I don't know how to thank you enough, really I don't. And please, do call me Laura. I've been out of my mind with worry —"

"Why didn't you report them missing?" Mandy blurted out. "We can't understand why no one's come for them till now."

"Mandy!" James exclaimed, looking horrified that she should dare to say such a thing — to Laura Dawson, of all people.

"I'm sorry," Mandy went on. "It's just that anything could have happened to the puppies, running around

London on their own. It's a miracle they weren't run over."

"But I only found out they were lost an hour ago!" Laura Dawson exclaimed, rubbing a hand anxiously across her forehead. "I came as soon as I could."

Mandy stared at her uncertainly. How could that possibly be true? They'd first seen Bruno at Buckingham Palace on Saturday — five days ago.

Penny came into the reception area. "You must be Ms. Dawson," she said, sounding very formal and just a little bit disapproving. "Would you like to come with me now, and I'll take you to the puppies?"

"Yes, of course!" Laura said, jumping to her feet. "Oh, I do hope they're mine — they've just got to be! You must let me explain —"

"Why don't we talk on the way over?" Penny said, holding the door open. "I'm sure you'd like to see the dogs as soon as possible."

"Can everybody else come along?" Laura asked. "I've got so many questions to ask."

"I'll stay and wait for you here," Dr. Adam volunteered. "It might be better not to have too many people crowding around."

Penny led the way down the corridor, and Mandy, James, and Casey followed behind with Laura Dawson.

"How come you just discovered the puppies were

missing?" Mandy asked her as they were walking. Laura was so warm and friendly, she didn't feel intimidated by her at all.

"Because I've been away on a publicity tour and didn't get back till this morning," Ms. Dawson replied, hoisting up her enormous bag as it slid down one shoulder. "I've been giving interviews about my new series and signing copies — all that commotion."

"Every Living Thing, you mean?" James asked, his eyes shining excitedly behind the glasses. "I've got the first book at home. It's fabulous!"

"I'm glad you like it," Laura Dawson replied with a quick smile. "Well, I went away on Saturday and left the dogs at home with my housekeeper. Apparently, she gave them a bath and took their collars off." She patted her bag and added, "I've brought them with me, and their leashes, too. Oh, I hope these really are my puppies!" She paused and bit her lip before carrying on. "Anyway, they were running around the yard to dry off in the sun, and the side gate had been left open. That must be how they escaped."

"And your housekeeper didn't let you know?" Casey asked. "Or report it to the police?"

"She thought she could find them on her own before I got back, and then I'd never need to know," Laura replied. "She kept calling the police to see if anyone had brought them in, but she wouldn't leave her details in case I heard of it. And she didn't think to contact the shelter, I'm afraid."

"Well, here we are," Penny said as she opened the door to the holding kennel. "Let's hope the story has a happy ending." Suddenly, the air exploded into a frenzy of barks and whines as the dogs inside greeted their visitors.

"We call them Nelson and Bruno," Penny went on, walking toward the puppies' cage, "though you may be able to tell us what their real names are."

Laura Dawson followed Penny. Mandy realized she could hardly bear to look at the cage, in case she discovered the puppies inside belonged to someone else. Nelson had rushed up to the wire and was standing there, wagging his tail, while Bruno hung back behind him. As soon as they saw Laura, they burst into high-pitched, excited barks, throwing themselves against the door in their eagerness to get at her.

"Oh, yes!" she exclaimed, crouching down to their level. "These are mine — George and Henry! Thank goodness they're safe!" Penny opened the cage door, and the two little dogs rushed out into Laura's waiting arms, nearly knocking her over in their excitement. "Stop it! Enough!" she laughed as they tried to lick every inch of her face.

"That's wonderful!" Mandy said, swapping delighted smiles with James and Casey as they watched the happy reunion. There could be no doubt at all that these were Laura Dawson's puppies and that they were as overjoyed to see her as she was to find them.

"So where's Princess?" Laura asked, looking up at Penny as the two dogs tumbled over each other in her lap. "Is this cage too small for three? Are you keeping her somewhere else?"

"I'm sorry?" Penny said blankly. "Who's Princess? These are the only Labrador puppies we have."

Mandy felt a cold chill sink into her stomach. She saw the joy in Laura's face slowly fade as she stammered, "But I have three dogs — George, Henry, and Princess. Didn't you find them all together?"

"No, I'm afraid we didn't," Mandy replied, kneeling down beside Laura and trying to calm the puppies while she explained. "We saw one of the pups at Buckingham Palace first, on Saturday, and then we spotted one in Victoria Street the next day. But we only managed to catch this fellow on Monday, in St. James's Park. He's the one we called Bruno." And she pointed to the more timid of the two pups.

"That's Henry," Laura said, hugging him to her. "So he was all on his own?"

"Yes! We didn't find his brother until this morning, in

Trafalgar Square," Mandy said. "At first, we thought he was Bruno — I mean, Henry — who'd escaped from the shelter. We didn't realize there were two puppies."

"And we had no idea there were three!" James added. "Where on earth could Princess be?"

"That's what we'll have to figure out," Mandy said determinedly. "We've found George and Henry — now we have to find their sister!"

"The thing is, we don't know which puppy we saw where," Mandy said, looking at the circle of intent faces around the table. The two Labrador pups had been checked out of the shelter, and now everyone was back in the café, trying to decide what to do next. Laura Dawson was sipping a cup of tea while Henry sat as close to her as he possibly could, resting his head on her lap. George lay on his back under the table, looking blissfully happy as James scratched his tummy.

"The puppies are so alike!" Mandy went on. "It could have been Princess we saw at Buckingham Palace or in Victoria Street, or maybe we haven't seen her at all. We just don't know!"

"Let's go through everything once again," Casey suggested. She turned to Laura. "The pups all escaped from your house on Saturday morning. And that's in Victoria Square, right? Just behind the Palace?"

"That's right," Laura answered distractedly. "And now it's Wednesday! It's awful to think of them being lost for all this time."

"Well, at least these two turned up safe and sound in the end," Dr. Adam said encouragingly. "Let's hope Princess will, too."

"Perhaps we should try to work out whether we might have seen her anywhere," Mandy said. "Is there anything unusual about her? Any distinguishing marks?"

Laura shook her head, as if trying to clear it. "She's a little bit smaller than her brothers," she said, petting Henry's ear. "But they do look very similar, chocolate brown all over." She thought for another few seconds and then said slowly, "There is one thing, I suppose. Princess has a real Labrador grin. You know how they seem to smile when they're pleased to see you? Well, she could smile for England."

"My photos!" James exclaimed, reaching inside his backpack. "Of course! Why didn't I think of that before?" He pulled out a pile of pictures and started leafing through them. "There!" he said, pulling out one of the early prints. "Do you recognize Princess? Could this be her?"

Laura Dawson fumbled in her bag and took out a pair of gold-rimmed glasses. She put them on and looked intently at the photo, while Mandy craned over her shoulder to see it, too. The little Labrador puppy gazed back out of the photograph at them, head to one side and one ear raised inquiringly. Mandy could just make out the tip of a pink tongue and the beginnings of a doggy smile.

"That's Princess!" Laura said delightedly. "No doubt about it — there she is." She took off her glasses and smiled as she put them back in her bag. "At Buckingham Palace, of all places!"

"Well, she has the right name for it," Dr. Adam said, taking a bite of his sandwich. "But that photo was taken a few days ago. I wonder where she is now?"

"She might still be there," Mandy suggested. She thought back to when they'd first seen the pup, bounding through the archway below the balcony and toward the grounds beyond. "After all, Buckingham Palace probably seems like paradise to her. According to James's guidebook, there are gardens at the back, with a lake."

"And these puppies do seem very adventurous," James added. "Remember where we found the other two."

"It's not exactly the easiest place to search, though, is it?" Casey said, draining her can of lemonade. "We can't just go up to the gate and say, 'Excuse me, Your Majesty, but we think our dog's in your garden. May we look for her?'"

"No, we can't," Mandy said, thinking hard. "But somebody we know is going to Buckingham Palace this afternoon, isn't she?"

"Mrs. Ponsonby!" James said, with a broad smile. "Of course!"

"Look, I don't want to pour cold water on your brilliant idea, Mandy," said her father, "but we don't even know what time Mrs. Ponsonby's supposed to be at Buckingham Palace. By the time we get over there, she may well have gone inside."

"Then I think we should wait for her to come out," Mandy said. "Oh, I know there's only a slim chance of finding Princess there, but it's worth a try, isn't it? And there's no way we could get inside the Palace ourselves."

"Well, we should be getting back to St. James's Park now," Dr. Adam said, looking at his watch again. "The others must be getting tired of waiting for us."

"I wish I could give you a ride," said Laura, standing up and untangling the puppies' leashes. They sprang to their feet, looking up at her expectantly as though they were eager to get home. "I couldn't possibly fit you all in my car, though." Then, fumbling in her bag, she said rather awkwardly, "I would like to offer you a reward for all the trouble you've taken. Please, would you accept a token of my gratitude?"

"Oh, no! Please don't," Mandy said, and saw her father was shaking his head, too. "It's been enough of a reward meeting you — and George and Henry, of course!"

"Well, then, at least let me pay for your taxi fares," Laura said, pressing a bill into Dr. Adam's hand, despite his protests. "I'd better get the puppies home now," she said, "but after I've made sure they're okay, why don't I come back and meet you outside the Palace? There must be something I can do to help."

"Fine," Mandy said. "We'll be there, however long it takes. Princess has got to be inside, I'm sure of it. We just have to find her and get her out. Or rather, Mrs. Ponsonby has to — though she doesn't know it yet!"

Eleven

"Just give us a little time. Please, Dad!" Mandy begged after the taxi had dropped them off on the sidewalk outside Buckingham Palace. "I'm sure Mrs. Ponsonby will be coming out soon."

"I'll meet you back here in half an hour," Dr. Adam replied, turning toward St. James's Park. "But no longer. We really can't expect Mom and the others to hang around in the park all day.

"If you three haven't found Mrs. Ponsonby by then, you'll have to give up," he added. "Don't worry, if the puppy is still somewhere around the Palace, I'm sure someone will find her sooner or later."

"So what does this Mrs. Ponsonby look like?" Casey asked when Dr. Adam had gone. She was looking at the steady stream of visitors coming out of a side exit. They were all smartly dressed, the men in dark suits and the women in flowery dresses and hats.

"She's pretty large, and she'll be wearing a hat with pink-and-purple ostrich feathers," Mandy said. She'd heard Mrs. Ponsonby describe her garden party outfit a hundred times. "It should be fairly easy to spot her. And she'll have a little Pekingese dog with her, too."

A few minutes later, there was a shout from Casey. "There's the hat!" she cried as the pink-and-purple-feathered creation bobbed toward them through the crowd. "You can't miss it. There's no sign of a dog, though."

"Mrs. Ponsonby!" Mandy cried, rushing up to her, with James and Casey close behind. "Thank goodness we've found you. Please, we need your help!"

"Is there anything the matter?" James asked, for Mrs. Ponsonby was looking decidedly cross. Her face was flushed, and she was frowning as she marched along. Casey stared at her in amazement.

"I was not allowed to bring Pandora to the garden party," Mrs. Ponsonby said indignantly. "I had to take her back to my hotel, and she was most upset about being left behind. By the time I returned to the Palace, I'd lost my place in line, and all the chocolate cake was gone. And I only caught the merest glimpse of royalty!"

"Oh, dear, that's a shame," Mandy said, trying not to sound too impatient. "But please, we really need you to go back —"

"There was no earthly reason why Pandora could not have accompanied me," Mrs. Ponsonby went on. "The party was held outside, after all. And on top of everything else, there was a puppy running around the Palace gardens! A puppy — just like the one you found in the park! Not wearing a collar, and quite out of control. Nobody could catch it."

"Yes!" Mandy cried triumphantly. "The puppy! That's why we need you to help us. Oh, please, Mrs. Ponsonby, could you go back and find the puppy for us? You see, we know who her owner is, and she's coming here any minute."

"Then I shall give her a severe talking to!" Mrs. Ponsonby retorted. "It's quite ridiculous, letting these young dogs cavort about all over London. What can she be thinking of?"

"It's a long story," Mandy said, "but it really isn't her fault. She's Laura Dawson, a famous writer, and she's so worried about her puppy. Just imagine how you'd feel if Pandora or Toby got lost."

"You're the only one of us who can get into the Palace

gardens, Mrs. Ponsonby," James added. "Please say you'll help! Laura Dawson will be so grateful."

Mrs. Ponsonby thought it over. "I will help you," she said eventually, "for the sake of the puppy. And because I am aware that duty goes hand in hand with privilege. Luckily, I still have Pandora's leash in my bag. Wait for me here. I shall return!"

"Well!" said Casey, wide-eyed, as Mrs. Ponsonby and her feathers sailed away. "She is something else!"

"Has there been any news?" Laura Dawson said, rushing up to Mandy, James, and Casey as they waited in a huddle on the pavement. "Have you seen your friend? And what are you doing on your own? Where's your father?"

"Princess is in the Palace gardens!" Mandy told her excitedly. "Mrs. Ponsonby saw her there. She's gone back in to see whether she can get her out, but it's been about twenty minutes, and there's no sign of her yet. Oh, and Dad's in the park with everyone else. They should all be coming back here any minute."

"How wonderful!" Laura exclaimed. "That means we're nearly there. George and Henry are safe at home, just around the corner. If only this Mrs. Ponsonby can rescue Princess, they'll all be together again! I can't dare to hope —"

"She's kind of a dragon," Casey warned her. "She might give you her views on puppies running around without collars."

"Oh, I don't mind that," Laura said with a sigh. "It'll be worth it to have Princess back. And besides, in a way she's right. I know I should have had the puppies microchipped, in case something like this happened. I'm going to make an appointment with the vet right away."

"Good idea," said Mandy. "It *is* worth it, and it won't hurt them at all."

Casey broke into their conversation. "There's Mom and Dad!" she said, pointing across the road. "And your parents, too — and all the others. Looks like they've had enough of waiting for us."

"Any luck?" Dr. Emily Hope asked as they all met on the sidewalk. "We really should be moving along now, Mandy."

"Oh, Mom, Dad! We're almost there!" Mandy said urgently. "Mrs. Ponsonby's seen Princess, and she's gone back inside the Palace gardens to find her. Please, we have to wait until she comes out again!"

Hurriedly, she introduced Laura Dawson to everyone before turning back to search for some sign of Mrs. Ponsonby coming out of the side gate.

"We've heard all about the puppies," Mandy's grandmother said. "But the thing is, we all have presents to buy before we go back to Welford tomorrow. Why don't we give Mrs. Ponsonby a call tonight to find out what happened?"

"I'm perfectly happy to stay here on my own," Laura Dawson added. "You've all done so much already."

"Oh, please — can't we wait a little longer?" Mandy pleaded. "This may be the only chance we have to see Princess." She just couldn't bear the thought of leaving the Palace without knowing whether the last puppy had been found.

"I know!" James said. "Why don't you go shopping here, in the Queen's Gallery, next to the Royal Mews? Don't you remember, Mandy? We stopped in there on Monday."

"Of course!" Mandy seized on the idea eagerly. "They sell all kinds of things there — books, china and glass, and chocolates and cookies with Buckingham Palace on them. And model soldiers, too. Your great-grandson Tommy would like those, Mr. Pickard."

"That sounds perfect," Dr. Adam said. "Nice and close by, and we can get all our shopping done in one fell swoop."

They all agreed. Everyone who wanted to shop went off to the Queen's Gallery, and Mandy, James, and Casey had another half hour to wait with Laura for news of Princess.

"Oh, come on, Mrs. Ponsonby," Mandy muttered under her breath. "Do your best!" What was happening behind those tall iron railings? Had Princess run off again? Had she been taken somewhere else?

Another fifteen minutes passed as they all waited anxiously, too tense to talk much. And then at last, Casey let out a cheer. "I spy the hat!" she shouted. "There she is!"

Behind the tall railings, the pink-and-purple feathers of Mrs. Ponsonby's hat seemed to shine triumphantly as she advanced toward them. A Palace official opened the gate to let her through.

"Is Princess with her?" Mandy called urgently. "Can anyone see?"

"Yes, she is!" Casey shouted, throwing her baseball cap in the air. "Oh, good old Mrs. Ponsonby! She's done it!"

"Princess!" Laura Dawson called, crouching down and throwing her arms wide open. "Come on, girl!"

Mrs. Ponsonby bent down to slip Pandora's leash from around Princess's neck. And then, in a streak of brown fur, the last little chocolate Labrador puppy came bounding across the pavement toward her owner.

"Oh, thank you, Mrs. Ponsonby!" Mandy cried, taking her hand and pumping it up and down in her excitement. "Thank you for finding Princess. How did you do it?"

"I applied my knowledge of dog psychology," Mrs. Ponsonby said modestly. "And then I tempted her out with a ham sandwich."

"I'm so grateful to you all," Laura said, smiling as broadly as Princess. She buckled the puppy's collar and clipped on her leash before standing up, the puppy in her arms. "If you won't accept any reward, then I insist on taking you all out, just as soon as Princess is safely back home. How about tea at the Ritz Hotel?"

"Tea at the Ritz!" Casey said, her eyes shining. "This day is just getting better and better. Wait till I tell Mom and Dad!"

Mandy gave Princess a hug, and the little dog licked her hand. She looked thin and dirty, but otherwise she seemed to be fine. "So what have you been up to inside Buckingham Palace?" Mandy asked, taking the puppy's head in her hands and gazing into her beautiful brown eyes. Then she turned to Laura Dawson. "You ought to write about Princess's adventures in your next book," she said. "They'd make a great story."

Laura Dawson laughed." Come on, Mandy!" she replied. "A pup at the Palace? Now, who'd believe that?"

TM

Look for the next
Animal Ark TM *book:*

MARE IN THE MEADOW

Mrs. Tandy took James and Mandy into the stable to show them where everything was, while Dr. Emily made friends with Chamomile outside. The mare's tack was on the other side of a partition, together with a fleecy numnah — a cloth to go under the saddle — and a grooming kit in a plastic container: some brushes, sponges, cloths, rubber currycombs, and a couple of hoof picks. There was also a halter with a rope attached to it. A riding hat that must have been Laura's stood on a shelf, but James and Mandy had brought their own.

"Great!" Mandy said, picking up the halter. "We can

tie Chamomile to something and give her a quick brush before we saddle her up. It looks like she's been rolling in the dirt."

James took the grooming kit and they went back outside. Mrs. Tandy showed them a ring on the stable wall where they could tether Chamomile. With the help of a couple more peppermints, Mandy had soon slipped the halter over the mare's head and she was safely secured. James chose a body brush for himself, passed one over to Mandy, and began to tackle a patch of mud on the mare's flanks.

"You can tell she's got a lovely temperament," Dr. Emily said admiringly, stroking the horse's bowed neck. "See how patiently she's standing!"

"And she's healthy, too, isn't she, Mom?" Mandy asked.

"Looks like it," Dr. Emily replied, running her hands down Chamomile's foreleg. "I checked her teeth just now and they're in good condition." She picked up Chamomile's leg and examined her hoof carefully before letting it rest back down on the ground.

"I'm just worried she's going to get bored on her own in this field all day," Mrs. Tandy said. "Laura used to ride her most days after work, you see. She kept her at a stable, but she fed and mucked her out herself. There's no way we can afford to keep her at full livery while Laura's away, but I can't really manage her on my own."

"We'll come as often as we can," Mandy began, but then she caught James's warning look and bit her tongue. He was right — they lived too far away and were too busy with other commitments to be of much help. It would be a mistake to make Mrs. Tandy feel she could rely on them, and then let her down. She began to brush Chamomile's coat with smooth, sweeping strokes. Well, they were here now. And at least for today they could give Chamomile a thorough grooming, and as long a ride as she wanted. That would be a pleasure!

"Now, you're sure you'll be OK, love?" Mandy's mom asked her as she and Mrs. Tandy prepared to go back to the house.

"We'll be fine," Mandy said confidently, giving the mare's mane a final comb. "We'll take Chamomile around the meadow first, just to get used to her — but you've seen how sweet and steady she is, haven't you?"

"Yes, you're right. Well, have a great time then," said Dr. Emily, giving her a quick kiss good-bye. "Mrs. Tandy's going to drop you and James back home when you've finished. Now, who's going first?"

"That'll be me," Mandy said, leading Chamomile over to the mounting block near the water trough that Mrs. Tandy had pointed out earlier. She held the reins bunched loosely in her left hand, stuck her left foot in the stirrup, and started hauling herself up onto Chamomile's back while James pulled down on the opposite stirrup, to stop the saddle from slipping. Chamomile stood quietly while Mandy got herself organized — tightening the girth and shortening the stirrups a couple of notches. Then she took up the reins, squeezed her heels against the mare's sides, and they were off!

Chamomile was wonderfully smooth to ride, and Mandy found herself grinning broadly as they walked around the edge of the field at a brisk, collected pace. She shortened the reins a little, gave the lightest touch with her heels, and the mare immediately broke into the balanced, comfortable trot they had seen earlier. Mandy waved triumphantly, and her mother and Mrs. Tandy waved back, before turning to leave the field.

"Good girl," Mandy said as she adjusted to the rhythm of Chamomile's trot, patting her neck encouragingly. The mare's ears flicked back and forth and she whinnied and shook her blond mane, as if to say that she was really enjoying herself, too.

Mandy looked around to give James a thumbs-up when, all of a sudden, she caught sight of someone staring down at her and Chamomile from an upstairs room in one of the houses that overlooked the meadow. A girl, maybe her own age or a little older, was standing by the window and watching intently as they trotted around the field. Because the houses were so close, Mandy could see her face quite clearly. Something about the girl's expression made her feel uneasy. She had been going to wave, because she was enjoying the ride so much and wanted to share her high spirits, but now she dropped her hand awkwardly.

Just then, Chamomile stumbled over a tussock of grass and Mandy lost her stride. By the time she looked back up at the window again, the girl had vanished.